Ropes & Roses

Cameron Hart

Published by Cameron Hart, 2024.

Want a free book?

Sign up for my newsletter[1] and get your free copy of Chasing Stacy!

One look at the stunning waitress carrying the weight of the world on her shoulders, and I'm a goner. I wasn't looking for a sweet little thing with auburn hair and more baggage than I can fit on the back of my bike, but there's no going back now. She's mine. I'll prove to her I'm more than capable of handling her past and making her feel safe again.

---

1. https://dl.bookfunnel.com/7wbqvhsx8r

Connect with me!

Check out my website, cameronhart.net[2], for sneak previews on my latest projects.

Follow me on social media:

Facebook Page - facebook.com/cameronhartauthor
Instagram - instagram.com/cameron.hart.author
TikTok - tiktok.com/@author.cameron.hart
Goodreads - goodreads.com/16081533.Cameron_Hart
Bookbub - bookbub.com/authors/cameron-hart

---

2. https://cameronhart.net/

Chapter 1

Shiloh

"Shiloh, don't forget your bus pass!"

"Dang it," I mutter under my breath as I turn on my heel and dash to the kitchen. "Thanks, Margaret," I say in a rush as I grab it out of her hand and head toward the door.

"Rent is due next week," she reminds me, flicking the end of her cigarette in the dirty ashtray. I hate that she smokes, but it's her apartment we're living in, so I keep my mouth shut and make sure to air out my room.

"I know, I'm working on it."

"Well, work a little harder. We were almost late last month."

I bite my tongue and barely suppress my eye roll. She says *we* as if she's contributed anything to the bills since I moved in three years ago. I already had a job at the local flower shop, which I still have and still love. When Aunt Margaret took me in after my mom died, she seemed a little too eager. I found out later it was because whoever was my guardian had control of the money Mom left me in her will until my twenty-first birthday.

It wasn't much, and now it's nothing. She spent it all and then asked me for more. I didn't have much of a choice but to keep working and help her pay the bills. Where else was I going to go? Now, here I am at nineteen, still trapped in this apartment. I have dreams though. Big dreams. I just need to somehow save money while keeping us afloat.

"I said I'm working on it." I grit my teeth but keep my composure. She loves getting a rise out of me, though I have no idea why. Maybe she's bored from sitting on her ass all day and watching soap operas.

Margaret gives me a fake sad smile, even pushing out her bottom lip in a pout. "You know I'd work if I could. My back though..." She winces over-dramatically and rubs her lower back. Last month it was her shoulder. She always has an excuse for why she can't pitch in, even though I've told her about work-from-home jobs.

"I know. Look, I'm really late this time," I say, backing out of the kitchen. Not only is her acrid cigarette smoke getting to me, but if I stay any longer, I might say something I regret. *Just a little longer*, I remind myself. How much longer, I don't know. But like I said, I have dreams.

Running outside, I make it to the corner of our street just in time to see the city bus pull out into traffic. "Noooo," I groan, pulling out my phone to see when the next bus comes. Fifteen minutes isn't too bad of a wait, but it will definitely make me late to my second job at the glamorous Joe's Hot Dog Shack.

I've only been working at The Shack for a few weeks, but I need this job if I ever want to save up enough to buy my floral shop. That's my grand plan. Monday through Friday, seven to three, I work at Love Blooms, a small but charming flower boutique. I love every second of being surrounded by such delicate beauty, even if some of the customers get on my nerves.

Joe's Hot Dog Shack, on the other hand, has been one long, miserable experience. And I haven't even worked there for a whole month yet. However, of the dozens of places I applied for a second job, they were the only place that had availability on nights and weekends. Joe himself is a bit of a jerk, but the pay is fair and the hours fit my schedule, so this is just what I have to do for the next... God, five years? Ten? Twenty?

I take a deep breath and try to pull myself out of my downward spiral.

Growing up, it was just my mom and me. My dad apparently stuck around for a bit but left when I was a few months old. Mom was only seventeen when she had me, and we were always more like best friends than mother and daughter. She was my whole world. Three years ago, when I was sixteen, my mom had an aneurysm in her sleep and never woke up. At least the doctors said it was a peaceful way to go, but those words aren't very comforting when your whole world is falling apart.

I arrived at my aunt's house penniless, homeless, and broken. While I don't love my life with Margaret, I'm no longer homeless, and I'm working on not being penniless too. As for the broken part... well, I think a part of me will always be missing.

The grief still gnaws at my heart, the emptiness spreading throughout my being and threatening to take over on the bad days. Sometimes I fear I might never heal from my devastating and unexpected loss.

I never want to experience that kind of pain again, which is why I don't let people get too close. I don't want to depend on someone only for the universe to take them away from me. It's been easy to keep my distance from Margaret. Aside from opening her home to me, she's done me no favors.

"You getting in, lady?"

I snap my head up, staring at the bus driver through the open door. I was so lost in my thoughts, I didn't notice the bus pulling up to the stop. I nod my head and step inside, sighing as I plop down on the nearest seat. Looking at my phone, I groan and see I'm already ten minutes late. Crap.

I nearly trip down the stairs as I get out at my stop, but manage to get my footing before I make a fool out of myself. I take off running down the block to The Shack, huffing and puffing the whole way. I can't remember the last time I ran. My stance on running is that it's only for when you're late or being chased by a psycho killer.

Bursting through the back door, I double over, placing my hands on my knees as I try to catch my breath.

"About time, Shiloh," Joe grunts from somewhere behind me. He smells like onions, and I have a sneaking suspicion he smells like that even when he isn't working.

"Sorry," I manage to say in between breaths, slowly turning to face him. The short, rotund man is starting to go bald, though his beard is full, if not a little matted. "I missed my bus and—"

"Don't care," he says, waving his hand in the air as if to swat away my excuse. "Got a special job for you today. It'll help remind you to be on time for your shifts. Tardiness earns you a day in the suit."

"The suit?" Oh God, what torture does he have in mind for me?

Joe walks a couple steps into his office and digs around a bin in the corner for a few moments before pulling out the most hideous hot dog costume. It's filthy, almost mangy, if that's even possible. One look and I know it hasn't been washed in a good long while. When he shoves it into my arms, the smell of stale sweat, cigarettes, and other unpleasant scents assault my nostrils, confirming my suspicions.

"The suit," Joe says with a sadistic smirk. His one gold tooth shines under the fluorescent lights, making him look like a thug with his unkempt beard. "Put it on and then grab a tray of samples. Diego will have it ready for you in the kitchen when you're done changing. You'll be outside today handing out hot dogs, girl."

He doesn't give me a chance to respond before he stomps away to yell at someone else.

I look down at the disgusting garment in my hands, scrunching up my nose. I seriously consider walking out and quitting, but the extra income is too good to pass up.

Sighing, I accept my fate and go to the bathroom to change.

It takes far too long to squeeze myself into the ridiculous outfit, and when I do, I look nearly scandalous. The main part of the hot dog suit is a brown spandex leotard of sorts. It extends down into shorts, though they hit very high on my thigh and might as well be underwear for as much as they cover.

The top of the leotard stretches obscenely over my breasts, making me all kinds of uncomfortable. This whole thing is uncomfortable, and not just because of the smell or the humiliation I'm sure to endure outside. I'm a thick girl with wide hips, a huge ass, and breasts to match. I never put myself on display like this, preferring jeans and baggy T-shirts to hide my curves.

Tears sting the back of my eyes as I stare at myself in the mirror. All I see are rolls and bulges, and it makes me feel even more ridiculous. I mean, I'm sure no one looks good in a hot dog suit, but this is next level.

The one good thing about the suit is that the bun part, which slips on like a puffy jacket, covers up my butt so my cheeks aren't hanging out of the mini shorts. I guess this is as good as it's going to get.

Taking one last fortifying breath, I square my shoulders and hold my head up high. It's hard to be a proud hot dog, but I'm going to do my damnedest to try. Joe wants to put me through the paces? Fine. I'll show him I'm made of tougher stuff than he thinks. When it comes to chasing my dream of owning a floral shop, there isn't much I wouldn't do.

I swing open the door to the bathroom with a renewed sense of purpose, only to run right into Denise. The flawless, long-legged blonde bombshell takes one look at me and starts laughing. "Hey Steve! Get a load of this!"

I roll my eyes and push past her, not letting her see my mortified blush. Diego calls out for me from the kitchen, letting me know he has my sample tray ready. I grab it and make a point not to look at anyone as I make my way outside.

It's only half-past eleven in the morning, but summer in Chicago means it's already sweltering outside. The heat is even worse out here with the sun beating down on me and bouncing off the pavement, warming my feet through my worn-out sneakers.

After about five minutes, I'm already sweating through the stupid costume. The Saturday foot traffic here in downtown is as bustling as ever and I get a few takers for the free samples. More often than not, however, people take one look at my plus-sized self stuffed into this hot dog suit and either gawk or try to hide their smirks. Some people don't even try very hard.

"I didn't know Joe's was serving jumbo-sized hot dogs," one man says as he and his friends approach. They are college kids, probably just a few years older than me. One of his bros snickers and slaps him on the back, encouraging him.

"Sample?" I ask, hoping they will go away once they get their free food.

"Are you offering yourself, wiener girl?" he mocks. "Cuz I don't do fat chicks."

My face is already dripping with sweat, but my cheeks manage to blush anyway, shame coursing through me at his words.

"Whatever, you would totally do a cow if it offered itself, man," another friend jokes.

"Fuck you, dude. Did you see the chick I took home from the bar last night?"

The three of them wander off, their conversation about last night's conquests fading into the background.

"Assholes," I mutter, rolling my eyes at them. Truthfully, their words tear at my self-esteem, which was already at an all-time low, thanks to the spandex currently giving me a wedgie and crushing my boobs. The fabric clings to every curve, roll, and imperfection. And I'm standing on a busy street corner, drawing as much attention to my flaws as possible in this obnoxious outfit.

I discreetly wipe my brow and brush away the hair stuck to my sweaty forehead. How long have I been out here? Twenty minutes? Ten hours? All I know is it's freaking hot as Hades, and I feel exposed and humiliated. How could Joe think this would help business? If anything, it's driving people away.

A gorgeous woman walks by, holding hands with her two kids. She's classy and sophisticated and reeks of money. The little boy on her right tugs on his mom's arm and pulls her in my direction. Dang it. The woman eyes me up, not caring one bit about hiding her disdain for me.

"Sample?" I offer, holding the half-empty tray out.

"Yes!" the boy with dark brown hair squeals.

"No, honey. We don't eat that kind of garbage."

The boy pouts and the woman whispers something in his ear. They both look at me and I can guess what she told him. *We don't eat that kind of garbage or else we'll end up looking like her.*

I do my best to glare at her, but it's only to cover up my tears. She power walks away from me with her nose in the air, dragging her kids along with her.

Closing my eyes, I try to push back the overwhelming urge to cry and go hide under my covers for the rest of my life. God, I've been on the verge of tears all day and I swear one more embarrassing interaction is going to break the dam of barely held back emotion. This is certainly not how I thought my day would turn out.

"What've you got there, darlin'?" The deep, smooth voice rolls over me seconds before the scent of leather and peppermint fill my lungs.

The slight drawl in the way he stretched out the word *darlin'* sends a shiver down my spine and makes my skin erupt in goose bumps. My eyes are still closed and I hold my breath, waiting for him to make some snide comment like everyone else.

"You doin' alright, sweetheart?" he asks. His voice is softer this time, tinged with what couldn't possibly be concern.

I pry one eye open and then squeeze it shut again.

There's no way he's that gorgeous. I must be starting to hallucinate from the heat. That's a thing, right?

I test my theory, opening both eyes this time. Nope, he's still a six-foot-something GQ cowboy, boots, hat and all, with sparkling green eyes and a bright grin. He's so freaking handsome, it's unreal. With just a hint of stubble on his angular jaw, full lips pulled back to reveal straight white teeth, and long eyelashes framing his emerald eyes, his flawlessness makes it hard to breathe.

"Sample?" I squeak out pathetically. I try holding the tray out to him, but the man is so close I end up nudging him in his hard abs with the edge of the platter.

"You didn't answer my question, beautiful," he says with a stupidly sexy smirk. "You feelin' alright?"

"Um…" I tilt my head back—waaaay back—to look him in the eye. That was a mistake. They aren't just green, they have golden spots that reflect the sunlight and give such depth to his stare. I'm about to tell him I'm fine, but something about the sincerity I find in those endless emerald eyes makes me want to tell him the truth.

No, I'm not alright. I feel stuck scrambling to make a living, pay the bills, keep my aunt happy, and save enough money to buy my freedom. I'm just so damn tired all the time. I'm constantly pulled in different directions and I feel like I'll always be barely keeping my head above water.

The sun beats down on me and my stomach churns as thoughts race and swirl in my head. The beautiful stranger's eyes never leave mine, his brows furrowing with worry. He opens his perfect mouth to say something, but I can't hear him over the ringing in my ears.

My breathing becomes shallow and my heart beats a rapid rhythm against my rib cage. Black dots swim around the corners of my vision, the darkness closing in with each ragged breath. The world tilts and the last thing I remember before everything fades away is strong arms wrapping around me.

Chapter 2

Colton

"Whoa there, I've got you," I murmur as the sexy hot dog falls into my arms. Can't say I've ever found a hot dog attractive, but I have a feeling anything this woman wears will turn me hard as a fuckin' fence post.

The poor girl is burning up, sweat dripping down her forehead despite the ashen look spreading over her delicate features. I scoop her up and cradle her curvy little body against my chest, taking half a second to breathe her in. I get hints of the dirty costume she's wearing, but mostly I smell sweet lilacs and roses and something that's all her.

I leave the discarded tray of samples on the sidewalk and make my way into Joe's Hot Dog Shack, hoping to get her inside where it's nice and cool. Who thought it was a good idea to send this little lady outside in a suffocating costume on a day like today? It's damn near ninety-five degrees and humid as fuck.

We get a few stares from patrons and staff, but I glare at everyone and head toward what looks like a back room.

"What the hell is going on?" a raspy voice bellows from somewhere near the kitchen.

"She passed out from the heat," I growl, not liking the tone of this guy's voice. A moment later, a short, stout man steps in front of me, his gut peeking out from under the hem of his stained T-shirt. He looks greasy and sleazy, and I don't trust him one bit. My instincts are almost never wrong.

"She's just being dramatic," the man scoffs. "I put her out there because she showed up late and now she's looking for an easy way to get out of work."

Now, I'm usually a pretty easy-going guy. I'm known as the peacekeeper, the charmer, the one with an easy smile and a helping hand. While that's true, I can also be vicious when the occasion calls for it.

"You put her in danger is what you did," I grunt, the sound coming from somewhere deep in my gut. The man's eyes go wide as saucers and he instinctively takes a step back. "She's under my care now and will be taking the rest of the day off to recover."

This snaps him out of his daze. "Hold on, there, buddy. That's not your call to—"

"And if you're lucky, she won't press charges for hazardous working conditions. Did you even give her a break? How long was she out there?"

Anger flashes across his beady black eyes, and I can tell he's about to say something that will earn him a broken nose. He must think better of it, because he eventually grunts and nods, pointing me to the back room where employee lockers are.

The breathtaking woman stirs in my arms slightly, her brows furrowing as she sticks out her bottom lip in a pout. Christ, even in her disheveled state, she's the most gorgeous woman I've ever laid eyes on.

I make my way over to a couch in the corner of the room and reluctantly lay her down after slipping the puffy bun-like jacket off. I'd like to keep her locked in my embrace forever, but her needs come first, always. And right now she needs a cool rag and some water.

No sooner does her back hit the couch cushions than her eyes shoot open. She's not just beautiful, she's a fucking goddess with golden eyes. I've never seen a color quite like it. My heart stops as I watch confusion and fear battle it out in her mind. I try to soothe her with a soft smile. God, those eyes. I didn't get a good look at them before she passed out on me, but now that they're trained right on me, I can hardly take a breath.

"Wh-what...?" she breathes out, trying to sit up.

"Take it easy, darlin," I say in my most calming voice. I hover over her, wanting to touch her, to hold her, to reassure her she'll always be safe with me. But I know these thoughts and urges are crazy, or at least they would be to her.

As for me, I've always believed in love at first sight. My parents locked eyes across the dirt floor of a good old-fashioned Texas hoedown nearly four decades ago and got married later that week. My dad said he felt a monumental shift in his chest, like his heart was rearranging itself to make room for all the love they would share. The old sap. I ate it right up though and knew for certain it would be the same for me.

I'll admit, I didn't expect to find the love of my life passing out from heat exhaustion after handing out hot dog samples, but it doesn't matter now. She's mine. Now I just have to convince her.

"I... um, what am I doing here?" she whispers. Her eyes are still cloudy as she blinks unevenly.

"Taking a little rest," I respond, easing her back so she's lying down once again. That simple touch has me craving so much more, but I pull my hand away. This is not the time to picture ripping off her clothes and spreading those thick thighs so I can see if she tastes as sweet as she smells.

"But..."

"I'll get you some water," I say before she can protest.

I reluctantly step away from her, scanning the area until I spot a sink in a makeshift employee break room. Grabbing a mug from the cupboard, I fill it up and dash over to my woman, not wanting to leave her alone for a second longer than I need to.

She eyes me up suspiciously, adjusting herself on the couch so she's propped up a bit. I don't like the doubt I see in her amber eyes, but I know this all is a shock to her. I can already tell I'll need to be patient and ease her into our relationship. She's mine as much as I'm hers.

"Thanks," the beautiful woman murmurs, taking the glass of water. I watch as she takes careful sips until she empties the mug. I grunt in satisfaction at the simple way I provided for her. There's so much more where that came from.

"More?"

"I can get it myself," she rushes to say. Before I can stop her, the woman swings her legs over the couch and tries standing up. She's not as steady on her feet as she thought, and her knees tremble before giving out.

"I've got you, darlin'," I murmur, hauling her into my arms once more. "Just sit down and take a breath. Maybe I can help you get out of your costume?"

She pulls away from me and cranes her neck to meet my gaze. Shit, the fire I see glowing in those golden eyes has my dick pressing painfully against my zipper. The glare she gives me, however, has me rethinking what I said.

"I knew you were too good to be true," she mutters. "Am I a joke to you? Just because I'm in a hot dog suit doesn't mean you can treat me however you want. I'm a person underneath this thing, a person with feelings and insecurities, a person who can only take so much, and I..."

To my horror, she suddenly bursts into tears. I don't know what my girl has endured today, or any other day, for that matter, but I never want to see her cry again.

I wrap my arms around her and turn us slightly so I can sit down on the couch, taking her with me.

"What are you doing?" she sobs miserably.

"Holdin' you."

"But why?"

Why? Because the moment I saw you, I knew you were my future. Because my heart is inexplicably tied to yours, and when you hurt, I hurt. Because I need to touch you in some way to make sure I didn't dream you into existence.

Of course, I don't say any of that. It would be too much, too soon. I may be ready to jump in feet first and throw caution to the wind, but once again, I hold back. *Patience*, I remind myself.

"That's what you're supposed to do when women cry, isn't it?" I tease, giving her my signature grin. Her eyes narrow and her nostrils flare, and God, she's a vision. Even when she's pissed off.

She sniffs and wipes her tears, squaring her shoulders before responding. "Do you go around holding lots of crying women?" she spits out.

"None as beautiful as you," I say with a wink.

"Enough of this. I don't know what your game is, but I need to get back to work." She tries scrambling off my lap, but I keep my hold on her.

"You have the afternoon off. I could probably convince your asshat of a manager to give you tomorrow off as well. Just say the word, darlin.'"

"Excuse me?!" This time, she jerks out of my arms and stumbles out of my embrace. "That wasn't your call to make. I need this job. So, thank you for your assistance, but I've got it from here. I'm fine. Really."

What started off as a confident tongue lashing fades away toward the end, her voice cracking on the last word. The beautiful, sad, curvy little goddess wraps her arms around her waist, covering up as much of her body as possible. Her cheeks are flushed and she stares at her feet, clearly waiting for me to leave. No chance in hell.

I don't even know her name, but I feel her unease, her vulnerability down in the depths of my soul. She shifts from foot to foot, not saying anything else. I have to proceed with caution. One wrong move will send her runnin' for the hills.

"It's okay to not be fine, sweetheart," I say slowly, keeping my voice as soothing as possible. With my palms out, I carefully take a step closer to her, watching her every move. She really is like a little filly. Wild, skittish, and in need of a safe place to grow.

"I'm not your sweetheart." Her words say one thing, but her voice is unsteady, like she wants to put up a fight but is too damn tired.

"Then what's your name?" I ask, taking another step closer.

She hesitates for a second, then finally breathes out, "Shiloh."

"Shiloh," I repeat, tasting her name on my tongue and letting it sink down into my innermost being. "I'm Colton, and I really think you should have some more water. Would you do that for me?"

Shiloh doesn't say anything, but her body sways ever closer to mine.

"Please? I'll worry about you all day if you don't."

Her brow furrows once more as she flattens her lips and assesses me with those amber eyes. I don't know what she sees, but I pray she knows I'm not messing with her. She's not a joke to me, she's my whole damn world. It kills me to think anyone has treated her less than the angel she is.

"Fine," she finally relents. "I guess I'm kind of thirsty."

A victorious smile stretches across my face as I hold out my hand to her. Shiloh stares at it, then flicks her eyes up to mine. I'm stunned by the emotion I see just beneath that shield she keeps up at all times. She still doesn't quite believe that I mean what I say, but she's curious enough to trust me, just a little bit. I'll make sure she never regrets it.

Shiloh places her tiny hand in mine and I wrap my fingers around it, shivering at the contact. The little gasp that falls from her lips lets me know she felt it too. Whatever this connection is, it's real, visceral, and undeniable.

Guiding her back to the couch, I help her get situated before refilling her mug. This time, I also grab a clean washcloth and wet it down with cold water. Handing Shiloh the water, I sit down next to her and roll up the cloth, draping it over the back of her neck.

"That feels good," she admits softly, closing her eyes.

I gently massage her shoulders, encouraging her to tip her head forward so I rub her neck as well. She's so tense, though I don't think it's all from the situation today. The deep knots in her shoulders let me know my girl has been carrying the weight of the world for a long time now. She doesn't know it yet, but I'm here now to share the burden, whatever it is.

Shiloh relaxes more and more, leaning into my touch. I remove the now empty mug out of her hands and urge her to lean against me. She lets me wrap my arm around her shoulders and tuck her into my side. My woman sighs and melts against me, nestling her head between my neck and shoulder.

I breathe this moment in, knowing she's going to snap out of it soon and try to push me away. Not that I'll go anywhere. If she needs to put up a fight before surrendering, I'll be right here, taking everything she dishes out.

Sure enough, after a few blissful moments, Shiloh sits up and scoots away from me. She pats down her hair, tucking a few of the light brown strands behind her ear. "I'm feeling much better now," she murmurs. "So, um, thank you."

"Never thank me for taking care of you, Shiloh." She finally looks up, her golden gaze meeting mine. Her cheeks glow with the most adorable rosy blush as she twists her hands in her lap. I cover them with one of mine, gliding my thumb along her soft skin in a barely-there touch.

Shiloh looks at me like she can't quite figure me out, like maybe I'm still playing a trick on her. I know my time is up and if I stay any longer, I'm going to overwhelm her. As much as I want to toss her over my shoulder and take her back to my cabin, I can sense she needs some time and space to come to terms with meeting her soul mate.

"So, um, I should probably get back to work..."

"I really wish you'd take the rest of the day off, but I'll never force you to do anything." It damn near kills me to think of her going back outside, but I don't have the right to tell her what to do. Besides, I spoke the truth. I'm not a controlling bastard, though I feel the obsession taking hold of me even now. I can give her this though. This space to think about what happened between us.

"Maybe I can ask Joe if I can work the floor instead of going back outside," she offers, looking to me for approval. She's a mystery, my woman. Independent through and through, and yet she longs for someone else to take the burden. To call the shots sometimes and take responsibility. I can be that for her.

"That's a great idea, sweetheart." I smile in approval of the compromise. It may seem small, but it's a big deal to me. In such a short time, Shiloh is already softening. I know we've got a long way to go, but this is progress.

"Okay, well..." She takes a deep breath and gives me one last look before standing up. I stand with her, trying not to let my eyes slip down her curvy body on display for me underneath the tight fabric. "I'll go change out of this and talk to Joe. I-I...um, thanks," she stutters, looking away from me.

I reach out and cup her chin, guiding her lovely face back to mine. "What did I say, darlin'? No thanking me. Can I see you again, Shiloh?"

"Oh." She looks surprised, though I can't imagine why. She has to feel it too. She has to know we're inevitable. "I don't know if that's a good idea. I mean, I don't even know you and you've already seen me like this." Shiloh waves her hands up and down her body, and I can't help but follow the motion.

Fuck, her heavy breasts pull against the thin material and I can see her nipples poking through the fabric. I knew she had to feel something between us, even if her brain is having a hard time catching up. My gaze wanders down her curves, taking in her wide hips and thick thighs. I want nothing more than to sink my fingers into her supple flesh and squeeze, feeling her every-fucking-where.

"And as incredible as the view is, I don't like anyone else seeing it," I growl, all calmness gone from my voice.

"What... never mind. I'm changing anyway, like I said."

I nod, bringing my eyes back to hers. "So when can I see you again?" I ask, giving her my most charming grin.

For a moment, she considers my question. I see the wheels turning in her mind and I wish I knew what she was thinking. I'm sure she's trying to convince herself to stay away, but she's having a hard time letting me go. I can work with that.

Her golden eyes turn slightly darker as her pouty lips curl up into a mischievous smirk. Holy hell, I'm dizzy from all the blood rushing to my aching cock. I want to taste her little smile, lick it off her lips before diving in deep and kissing her with everything I am.

"I'll be here next Saturday from eleven to seven," she says with a playful sparkle in her eyes.

It's not the answer I wanted, but I'll take it. I have more resources than she thinks through my job at Watchdog Security.

She wants me to chase her? Game. Fucking. On.

Chapter 3

Shiloh

Usually, being surrounded by chrysanthemums, roses, and snapdragons calms me down and puts my mind at ease. I love the delicate scent of the flowers mixed with crisp water and wet earth. If I close my eyes and run my hands over the velvety petals of the nearest arrangement, it's almost like I'm walking through a mountain valley filled with sunshine.

Today, however, not even the new shipment of colorful gerbera daisies can distract me from thoughts of the mysterious, too-freaking-handsome GQ cowboy I met three days ago. *Colton*. Even just thinking his name has heat rushing to my cheeks... and other, lower areas of my body.

He wrapped his arms around me and held me close to his chest, letting me breathe in his earthy, leather scent mixed with sharp, tangy citrus. For a brief moment, my racing thoughts stilled, the responsibilities of my life vanished, and all that was left was the steady rise and fall of his chest as I curled into his embrace.

Why I felt safe and seen for the first time in forever is beyond me. I don't know Colton at all except that he apparently has a hero complex and can't help himself when there's a damsel in distress. Granted, a distressed hot dog might have been a new one for him, but Colton exudes protectiveness and authority, even when he's grinning so wide his dimples pop out.

And those eyes... they were the lightest green with hints of silver shining whenever he looked at me. Of course his hair was perfectly disheveled, a little long, but in that effortlessly sexy and somehow perfect way. As if that weren't enough to make a girl swoon, he carried my plus-sized self in his thick, strong arms as if I weighed no more than a feather. I won't lie, that was a huge freaking turn-on, but I had to shut that thought down immediately.

I'm still trying to figure out why the Greek god of a man took the time of day to make sure I was well-hydrated after my mortifying fainting spell. More than that, he held me while I had a complete meltdown, tears, snot, unattractive sobbing, and all.

His gentle, almost reverent touch still burns my skin every time I think about that day, as if he branded me. The past few nights, I can't stop thinking about the way he massaged my neck, kneading my sore muscles like he already knew my body better than I did.

Sitting right there next to him, soaking up Colton's warmth and strength, I almost forgot I was in a humiliating, degrading outfit. I almost forgot the pressure of doing whatever's necessary to pay the bills and survive one more paycheck. For one, brief, beautiful moment, I just... was. I simply existed in that second, locked in time with his green eyes and reassuring smile.

Something shifted deep in my chest. A piece of me chipped away, loosening the tightness in my shoulders and lungs. I could breathe easier, knowing as long as Colton was here, no harm would come to me.

But that had to come to an end sooner or later. Reality came flooding back into my awareness and I had to get a grip. It's not like Colton was going to pluck me out of my stagnant life and whisk me away to my happily ever after. So, I had to get ahead of whatever spell the charming cowboy was casting on me.

Three days later, and I still feel like I'm waking up from a dream. I'm not willing to admit it to myself yet, but I think... I think I might miss him. Ridiculous, I know. It's probably just a crush. I can't say I've ever had one before, but then again, I've never seen Colton before.

Is this giddy, nervous feeling what made all the girls in my high school fall all over themselves for guys who mostly ignored them? If so, I almost admire their strength. I've only been living with this tingly, intense infatuation for a few days and it's already driving me crazy. I don't know how other girls live through crushes and move on to someone else. Colton is all-consuming, and I've only spent a handful of moments with him.

A part of me regrets pushing him away by telling him he can see me at work next Saturday, but what else was I going to do? I don't expect him to show up, of course. I'm sure he's already forgotten about me. If he hasn't, it's only because he's been telling his friends about the hot dog girl who passed out in his arms. I bet they shared a laugh over a few beers.

The thought of Colton making fun of me makes my stomach drop as a heavy weight sits on my chest. Tears sting the back of my eyes, but I blink them away. I shouldn't care what he or his friends think of me.

"Ouch," I mutter, pulling my hand away from the arrangement I was working on. I suck on the tiny wound in my thumb from the thorn that pricked it. I'm angry at myself for getting lost in thoughts of Colton for the millionth time in the span of a few days. I thought I was made of stronger stuff than this and it frustrates me to no end that the first man to ever pay me any attention has my heart and mind tangled up in knots.

The bell above the door chimes, alerting me to a new customer. Thank goodness. I need to get my head in the game and stop thinking about...

"There you are, beautiful," Colton greets me, the adorable grin on his face begging to be returned.

"Oh, shit," I whisper, my mind blanking as my knees start to shake. I'm so startled by his presence, I forgot all about the vase in my hand. It drops to the floor, shattering and spilling water all over the place. "Crap," I mutter, heat immediately rushing to my face. Why can't I stop making a fool of myself in front of him?

I can't look at his tanned, muscled perfection while I'm covered in water and surrounded by a mess of petals, stems, and glass. Turning on my heel, I escape to the back room and grab a mop and broom. I take a few deep breaths, telling myself he'll surely have left by the time I get back out there. Why would he stick around after seeing what a spaz I am?

I've almost fully recovered by the time I make my way to the front to clean up my mess. When I get out there, however, Colton is crouched on the floor, picking up the flowers and setting them on the counter delicately.

God, he's somehow sexier than I remembered. He hasn't seen me yet, so I take a selfish moment to admire the most attractive man I've ever encountered. Though he's wearing a checkered button-down and Levis, I can see his muscles flexing underneath the material, giving me a delicious hint of what's beneath his shirt.

As if sensing me, Colton turns and looks at me over his shoulder, giving me that boyish grin of his. A million fireflies flutter in my belly and my heart beats a little too forcefully, causing me to gasp. Colton's features turn from charming to worried in an instant. His brows furrow as he stands and closes the distance between us.

"Did you hurt yourself, sweetheart?"

I tip my head back as he approaches, shivering when his hands cover my shoulders. Colton gently massages my sore muscles, just like he did the first time we met. His touch calms me in a soul-deep way I've never experienced. The feeling of safety washes over me once again, and some part of me knows Colton will always protect me.

Shaking my head, I do my best to clear away the crazy thoughts. I blink up at the tall, handsome cowboy, allowing myself to smile for half a second at his solid black Stetson. I don't come across many cowboys here in the city. If they all look like him, maybe that's for the best. My poor hormones are all over the place just knowing one such man exists. I don't think I could handle multiple Coltons in the world.

"Shiloh? You okay, darlin'?"

"Mmhm." I nod my head, completely hypnotized by his slight southern drawl. The way my name rolls off his tongue has me squeezing my thighs together. A sudden ache blooms in my lower belly, taking the place of the nervous, fluttering fireflies.

We stare at each other for a beat, and then Colton grabs the mop and broom from my hands and proceeds to clean everything up while I stand there and gape at him. Who is this guy and why is he always cleaning up my messes? What is he even doing here, anyway?

Then it hits me.

"I'll finish cleaning up while you pick out some flowers for your girlfriend," I say with more force than necessary. God, is that my voice? I sound bitter and almost jealous. I have no right to be, but the sudden image of Colton going home to a model-esque blonde with long legs and who knows how to put on makeup makes me sick to my stomach.

Here I am, tripping all over myself—quite literally—in this man's confusing, arousing presence, while he has a girlfriend waiting for him. Of course he does. Colton is dangerously sexy with rippling muscles, sparkling green eyes, and a smile that makes me feel like I'm the only person in the world. I'm sure he has women falling all over him. Women who are worldly, petite, and not clumsy. Women who are the opposite of me.

Colton straightens his back, freezing for a moment before standing up. He empties the last of the glass shards into a cardboard box before throwing the whole thing away. Slowly, the towering cowboy turns in my direction, his emerald eyes never leaving mine as he stalks toward me.

"Jealous, darlin'?" he drawls, that infuriatingly sexy smile curling up one side of his lips. I glare at him and ball my hands into fists, resting them on my hips. This only makes his little smirk grow as a fire roars to life beneath his glittering eyes.

"No," I huff out, taking a step back. "It's none of my business. What kind of flowers does she like?" I ask, turning away from him and busying myself with one of the arrangements lining the shelves.

I pull out one of the daisies and then stick it back into the vase, fluffing the leaves a bit to fill in empty space. There's nothing wrong with the flowers, but I can't look at Colton while he tells me about his girlfriend. I'm not jealous. I'm not. I just don't think whoever he's with is good enough. She probably doesn't appreciate his good nature. I bet she's a shallow, horrible shrew.

I'm about to grab one of our most expensive arrangements and shove it in his chest just so he'll leave, but then the heat of his body covers my back. I freeze, holding my breath and trying not to shiver from his presence.

Colton gathers my hair in his hand and gently rests it over my shoulder, his fingers trailing down my neck. I gasp softly when he leans down, replacing his fingers with his lips. Colton presses feather-light kisses across my exposed shoulder and up my neck, nipping at a sensitive spot just beneath my ear.

"There's no one but you, darlin'," he murmurs, brushing his soft lips against the shell of my ear. "Only you, Shiloh."

Against my better judgment, I relax against his chest, tilting my head back to rest on his shoulder. Colton nuzzles into the side of my neck and wraps his arms around my waist, not caring that my apron is still soaking wet from the flowers. He spreads his hand out over my stomach, pressing me closer, closer, closer, like he can't get enough.

We're suspended in this moment, my cowboy holding me while I soak up every bit of strength he's giving me. Just like the first time we met, his warmth and steady heartbeat settles me down, silently banishing my doubts and fears.

Colton presses his lips to my temple, breathing me in before kissing me there. To my great disappointment, he steps away from me. Cold rushes down my spine, replacing the comforting heat of being near such a powerful man.

I grip the shelf in front of me, kicking myself for letting him affect me like this. What did he mean? *Only you, Shiloh.* We hardly know each other, and what he's seen of me isn't exactly flattering. In fact, the whole hot dog suit incident was one of my more embarrassing moments, and I'm not sure there's a way to come back from that.

Taking a deep breath, I turn around and try laughing off his comment. Only, it comes out as some sort of snort-slash-shrill cackle. *Oh my God*, I groan internally.

Clearing my throat, I try again, this time managing to sound a little more human. "Right. So, uh... so what are you looking for today?" When he doesn't answer, I'm forced to tear my eyes away from my tattered shoes and look at him. Those green irises flash with something both sweet and playful. "What?" I ask, the silence stretching out the longer he stares at me.

Finally, Colton shakes his head, though that smile never leaves his lips. "You're just so damn beautiful," he says more to himself than to me.

"Um..." I'm not sure what to say to that. I've never had the attention of any man, let alone one who looks like Colton. "Okay. Thanks for that," I say awkwardly, stumbling over my words. He grins, making me blush and look away from the devastatingly handsome cowboy.

"Which flowers are your favorite?" Colton suddenly asks as he steps up next to me. He looks around the shop and I wonder what he sees. Shelves in need of repair? Chipped hardwood floors? Faded walls that could use a fresh coat of paint?

I can't explain why I want his approval so badly, especially since the shop isn't even mine yet. I have a list of things I want to spruce up if I ever save enough to buy this place from the owner, but it's just a dream at this point. One that feels fragile and scary and impossible all at the same time.

"We just got a fresh shipment of gerbera daisies," I answer, wiping my hands on my apron and heading over to the counter with said flowers. "They are bright and cheery, perfect for pretty much any occasion."

Colton doesn't even look at the giant blue daisy in my hand. Instead, his eyes are trained right on mine.

"O-or if you're in the mood for something a little classier, I have an arrangement of white and purple lilies," I press on, avoiding his gaze. "And this time of year we also have amazing tulips."

When I finally look up at Colton, his brows are slightly furrowed, his head tilted to the side as if he's trying to figure something out. "That's not what I asked, beautiful."

"Stop calling me that!" I blurt out. Slapping a hand over my mouth, I stare at him wide-eyed, unsure of where that outburst came from. "Sorry," I mutter, clearing my throat. *God, what is wrong with me?*

I spin around to try and hide from him again, but he loops his fingers around my wrist and lightly tugs me toward him. I stumble into his chest, taking a moment to breathe in his citrusy, leather scent.

Colton steadies me with a hand on my hip while his other hand cups my face. "I'll have to be more careful with you," he murmurs, stroking my cheek with his thumb. His eyes track the movement as a look of awe covers his face. It's almost like he's fascinated by the way I feel.

I open my mouth and then close it, once again at a loss for words.

Finally, Colton's eyes find mine, the blazing green fire calming down as he looks at me with all the care in the world. His concern for me almost has me falling into his arms and begging him to hold me again, but I manage to stand my ground.

"You have no idea how beautiful you are," he whispers. It's not a question, nor is it directed at me. It's like he's studying my every movement, breath, and thought, taking it all in and then digging for more.

"W-well, I..." What do I even say to that?

"Tell me, precious. What's your favorite flower?"

Precious. Does he really think I'm precious?

"It's silly," I whisper, surprised I answered him at all. I wasn't planning on saying anything, but my mouth had other ideas, apparently.

"Nothing about you is silly," Colton responds, lifting his hand away from my cheek so he can tuck a few strands of hair behind my ear. "Now tell me."

The deep, velvety tone of his voice sparks a fire in my core, one that quickly grows out of control. Flames lick my nerves, making me sensitive and aware of every place he's touching me.

"Roses," I sigh, looking down. "Cliché, right? I work with exotic flowers, elegant flowers, and rare, intricate flowers, yet my favorite will always be roses."

Colton rests his forehead on mine, then cups the back of my neck, keeping me close as his other hand slides to the small of my back. "Why roses?"

I feel more than hear his words as they tickle my skin. There's no judgment in his voice, just curiosity.

I'm trembling from his hands on me, and my mind is spinning, trying to figure out if I'm dreaming all this up or if he's playing a joke on me. As much as I want to push him away and hide in the back room until he leaves, a bigger part of me wants him to see me. Having his attention is addicting. I already know I'm going to miss him when he leaves.

"They were my mom's favorite," I tell him, my voice barely audible. I'm sure if he weren't mere inches from my face, he wouldn't have heard me. "She always said it would be a luxury to have fresh roses every day. We didn't have a whole lot of extra money for things like flowers or fancy treats. Instead, we'd draw what we would get each other if we won the lottery. I always drew roses," I say with a sad smile. "She kept all of them in an album on the coffee table," I muse, remembering the book of drawings.

Colton tightens his hold on me, massaging my neck while pressing me ever closer into his solid chest. Silence falls around us, though it's not uncomfortable. He's giving me space to either keep talking or let it go. I shock myself as much as him when I continue.

"I planted a rose bush for Mother's Day when I was fifteen," I whisper. I can't speak much louder for fear I'll break down into tears. "The first year was hell trying to figure out the proper pH balance for the soil, the perfect amount of sun, and how much water the rose bush needed. The second year, I got three blooms. They were beautiful."

"That's amazing, sweetheart," Colton says so gently. "I bet your mom was so proud of you."

A deep, familiar pain grips my heart, shrouding it with grief. "She passed away before she got to see them. I-it was so sudden. I d-didn't know... I didn't know..."

Colton wraps his arms around me, hauling me up into his chest. "I'm so sorry, baby," he coos. "I can tell how much she meant to you. How much she still means to you."

I nod my head before burying it into the side of his neck. I bite the inside of my cheek to keep from sobbing. I don't want to break down in front of this man twice. Once was bad enough.

He rocks me back and forth, whispering sweet, soothing words into my ear. I never want to leave his embrace. I could live right here, breathing him in, clinging to his carved muscles, and begging him to never leave.

And then reality slaps me in the face.

I'm already too close. How did Colton slip right under my defenses? He didn't even try that hard. I practically opened the door and put out a welcome mat. But I can't afford to let him get any closer. What if he leaves me? What if something happens to him? What if—

"I'm right here," he murmurs, stroking my hair.

How did he know what I was thinking?

"You're safe with me, Shiloh. My precious Shiloh."

Dammit, why does he have to say the sweetest things? It's nearly impossible to untangle myself from Colton's embrace, but I manage to step away from the confusing cowboy stirring up dangerous emotions in me.

"Anyway," I say, clearing my throat and wiping a few stray tears from my face. "Um, so... okay, well, I should go. To the back. Of the store. Because of... my job."

Ugh, shut up and leave already!

"Whatever you say, beautiful," Colton rasps, grabbing my hand up in his. He brings it to his lips, turning my hand over and pressing the lightest kiss to my palm. "I'm not giving up on you. Thank you for today."

I blink up at him, not sure what he means. I'm not sure what anything means anymore, only that Colton is trouble. He's got me thinking and feeling all kinds of things I don't know what to do with.

The tall, handsome cowboy leans down and kisses my cheek before turning around and walking out of the shop. Once again, I'm left gaping after him, wondering how on earth I'm going to resist him if he visits me again.

Chapter 4

Colton

My eyes snap open and I gasp for air, trying to cling to the last images of my dream. Shiloh was in the shower, dripping with soap and water, and giving me a heated stare. Of course, I had to join her.

I shut my eyes again and trail a hand down my chest and stomach, pausing for half a second before reaching into my boxers and wrapping my hand around my sore as fuck dick. Hissing at the contact, I throw my head back and close my eyes once again, allowing my fantasy to play out while I stroke myself.

Those golden eyes shine with mischief and lust as I step into the shower and smooth my hands down her curves. Christ, my balls draw up tight as I think about how soft and smooth her skin was when I cupped her cheek the other day. I'm sure she's soft all over. I can't wait to find out.

I imagine my woman looping her arms around my neck and pulling me down for a scorching, claiming, desperate kiss. I respond by gripping her thighs and wrapping them around me, walking her backward until she's pinned against the shower wall.

Groaning and squeezing my cock, I rub myself raw thinking about piercing her tight little cunt over and over, filling her up until she's shaking and screaming my name. I practically feel her fingernails dig into my skin, tearing me up the same way I'm tearing up her soaking wet pussy.

"Fuck," I growl, the sound almost guttural as I furiously pump my hand up and down my shaft. Sweat beads my forehead and every muscle in my body tenses, but I grit my teeth and hold back my orgasm. I don't want to let go of the fantasy just yet.

Imagining Shiloh's breathy whimpers against my lips as I rut into her is nearly my undoing. It's only when I picture her face twisted up in excruciating pleasure that I finally find my release. Cum splashes across my stomach in never-ending bursts, each one draining me of strength.

Finally, Jesus, finally I go limp, though my dick still twitches with the memory of the best orgasm I've ever had. And I haven't even kissed her yet. Lord, my precious girl might just be the end of me once I get inside her.

Gathering my wits about me, I roll over slightly and see it's just past seven in the morning. It's as good a time as any to get the day started.

I take my time in the shower, and yeah, I can't stop myself from getting off again to images of my curvy goddess riding my face while I stretch her tight little back entrance with my fingers. Jesus, I need to get a grip.

I smirk, laughing at my own play on words. I've got a grip, alright. Just not on my sanity.

Going through my morning routine, I get the coffee brewing and check my messages. My schedule is pretty flexible, especially since I don't have an assignment right now.

I'm part owner of Watchdog Protection, Inc., along with my buddies Logan and Slater. We all met serving in the Marines, though our military careers took us in different directions over the years. Logan was the first to get out, and I joined him a year or so later.

When Slater was honorably discharged after landing on a roadside bomb and fucking up his leg and shoulder, he was in bad shape, and not just physically. There's no doubt the seven-foot giant saw some shit on his last tour. The haunted, hollow look in his eyes said it all.

He scared the bejeezus out of me when he came back all broody and quiet. His pain is a palpable thing most days, though he never talks about it.

Logan and I stuck by him though. We even moved in briefly when Slater was released from the hospital, despite his many protests. He's still haunted by his demons, though having Watchdog has helped all of us settle and adjust to life as civilians.

It's been a few days since I've heard from Logan. He's out in Cali on an assignment for an old friend. Apparently the daughter has a stalker. Last time we talked, there was a close call with the stalker and the two of them needed to get to a safehouse. That's where I come in handy. I've got all sorts of connections, some more reputable than others. Either way, I'm the kind of guy who gets shit done, and knowing damn near everyone certainly helps.

I pull out my phone and call Logan, wanting to check in and get an update.

"Colton," comes his deep voice over the phone.

"Just seeing how you and the girl are holding up in the safehouse. You guys need anything?"

"Spencer," Logan grits out.

"Huh?"

"Her name. It's Spencer. Not *girl*."

He's angry, though I have no idea why.

"*My* girl," he mutters under his breath. That's when it hits me.

I'm glad Logan can't see my goofy grin, otherwise he'd probably try and knock it off my face. "My bad. How are you and *your* girl, Spencer?"

He doesn't answer at first, and for a second, I don't think he will. Then Logan lets out a sigh and chuckles. Holy shit, I don't think I've ever heard him laugh.

"We're good. Real good."

Before I can make fun of him, another voice filters through the line. It's a light, airy voice, obviously belonging to Spencer. "Everything okay?" she asks. I can picture Logan nodding and grunting. The woman giggles, and then there's some shuffling around and a deep groan.

"Okay, okay, I'll leave you two be," I say with a laugh, shaking my head the whole time. "So you guys are safe then? Has the threat been eliminated?"

"Yes," Logan pants. "Your buddies at Chaos MC helped out."

"Good, good. Now get off the phone before I throw up."

Logan laughs and Spencer gasps and then giggles. The line goes dead and I stare at my phone, not quite believing the stoic Logan found a woman who makes him laugh and kisses him breathless. Good for him. I hope they'll get along with Shiloh, because she's about to become the most important thing in my life.

Finishing up my coffee, I quickly get dressed, suddenly anxious to get to Shiloh. It's been far too long since I've been in her presence. It's Saturday, which means I know exactly where to find my woman. Hopefully her boss learned his lesson and didn't stick her outside today.

Fifteen minutes later, I'm pulling up to Joe's Hot Dog Shack. Of course it's not open yet. I don't know what I was thinking. It's barely eight in the morning. I bang my hands on the steering wheel, frustrated that I'll have to wait another few hours to see Shiloh.

After making a few phone calls and checking in on Slater, it's nearly eleven. Perfect. I pull into the parking lot once more, this time nearly giddy as I hop out. There's no doubt Shiloh is the one for me. I've never felt so alive, so happy, so absolutely excited just to see someone. I just pray she feels even a fraction of what I'm feeling. Even that much would be impossible to ignore.

I swing open the door, scanning the area for my beautiful Shiloh. A few waitresses in short shorts and tight shirts turn in my direction. I'm used to getting appreciative looks from women, but now their gazes feel wrong. The only person I want looking at me with lust-filled eyes is Shiloh. Where the hell is she?

A tiny gasp sounds from behind me, and I spin around, staring into a pair of magical golden eyes. Shiloh gapes at me and takes a step backward, but the heel of her worn-out sneakers catches on the floor, sending her tumbling.

The tub of silverware she was carrying drops to the ground with a dramatic thud, and I reach out just in time to steady Shiloh before she falls.

"You okay there, darlin'? Didn't mean to startle you."

She looks up at me, her eyes going wide as her cheeks turn the most adorable shade of pink. "It seems like you're always asking me that question. It's like you make me stupid and clumsy every time you're around."

Shiloh looks down, but I don't let her hide from me. Tipping her chin up with my nose, I give her what I hope is a disarming smile. "You're not stupid, baby. And I like that I fluster you a bit." She glares at me and I pull her closer, pressing her generous curves against my chest. Her breath comes out in shallow pants, and her pulse pounds against the side of her neck. I lean down, ghosting my lips over her trembling flesh before nibbling her ear. "I promise, beautiful, I'm far more shaken up than you are. You've changed my whole world and you have no idea."

"Wh-what?" Shiloh stares at me and then opens her mouth to ask another question. Unfortunately, her asshat of a boss decides to step in.

"Not you again," he grunts, looking me over.

I want to dent his face in with my fist, but instead, I tip my hat to him. "Just checking in on my girl. I accidentally startled her," I explain, not wanting her to get in trouble for dirtying up all that freshly wrapped silverware.

"That so?" Joe looks from me to Shiloh.

She gives me a questioning look, then slowly nods her head.

"Fine. Whatever. Shiloh, you know where the clean silverware is. Go wrap it up, start from scratch, and stick the dirty ones in the wash." Joe rolls his eyes, making me growl.

I don't like his rudeness or the way he dismisses Shiloh. In fact, I don't like anything about this prick and I want nothing more than to whisk Shiloh away and tell her she never has to work this shitty job ever again.

My girl is nothing if not independent though, and I don't think she'd appreciate me telling her what to do. As frustrating as it is not to throw her over my shoulder and have my wicked way with her, I respect the hell out of her wanting to make it on her own. I just wish she'd let me help.

I'm about to step in and offer to help, but Shiloh shoots me a look. How she knew what I was thinking is beyond me, but it's perfect. She shakes her head no, but I just wink at her. Those golden eyes flash with fire, and Christ, my cock throbs to life, instantly hard at the sight of her defiance.

Shiloh gathers the silverware, piling it into the tub before taking off for the back. I wait a few minutes, pretending to look over the menu before searching for the bathrooms. Just like I thought, the hall with the bathrooms also leads to a small backroom where I assume Shiloh was sent to rewrap the silverware.

I knock lightly and then push the door open. I can't stop the smile spreading out across my face at the sight of her. She's standing at a table in the back, sorting through silverware. In shorts and a casual T-shirt, my woman is stunning. She's trying to look annoyed with me, but I see her blush and the way she worries her bottom lip. Shiloh is fighting this for some reason, but she can't hide her body's response to me. It gives me hope.

"What are you doing back here?" she asks with narrowed eyes.

"Helping," I say with a shrug and a wink. I love seeing her cheeks turn from pink to crimson. I'll have to wink at her more often.

"I don't need your help, thanks," she says, brushing me off as she gives me her back.

I walk up behind her, caging her against the table with an arm on either side of her. Just like that day in the flower shop, she relaxes against me, letting me wrap my arms around her and hold her.

"It's okay to accept my help, beautiful. I have a feeling you've been carrying the weight of the world on your shoulders for far too long. Let me take care of you," I whisper, kissing the side of her neck.

"Why?" comes her breathy response.

"Why not?"

Shiloh spins around in my arms, though I think she misjudged how close we are. Her face is inches from mine, her sweet breath tickling my lips and tempting me beyond reason.

"Why me?" she asks again.

I grip her hip with one hand, groaning softly at how damn good her curves feel. My other hand slides around to the back of her neck, diving into her hair and wrapping it around my fingers. I tug lightly, tipping her head back and exposing more of her neck to me.

I can't stop myself from smelling her skin, nibbling on her neck, and licking the shell of her ear. My girl trembles in my arms, making me crazy with need. I suck on her pulse point, ready to sink my teeth into her flesh and mark her as mine. I somehow restrain myself. Not yet. I get the feeling she'd be embarrassed if I gave her a hickey at work. Shame.

"Why not you?" I respond, continuing to torture her with little licks and nibbles up and down her neck. God, she's so responsive, her entire body a livewire that sparks every time I touch her.

"Colton," she says exasperatedly. "You're not answering my question," she pouts. Fucking adorable.

"Maybe this will answer it, then," I murmur before dipping my head down and closing the distance between us. I give her a second to pull away, but she pleases me to no end when she leans forward and kisses me first.

Her taste wrecks me.

She's sweet and floral, but there's something there that's just... Shiloh.

She parts those precious lips of hers and lets me in, lets me drink more of her down, lets me become completely addicted to her. Never, in all my years, has one kiss so completely destroyed me.

And then she moans.

Softly at first, like she doesn't know if she should. Our tongues tangle as my hands slide up and down her body, over the curve of her breast, her ribcage, her waist, finally landing on her hips.

The little goddess writhes against me, her eager, inexperienced kiss driving me wild. I'm ravenous for her, utterly delusional with pleasure. I pull her toward me and slide my hands lower to her thighs, lifting Shiloh up onto the counter next to the tub of silverware. She moans loudly as we both get completely lost in this kiss.

I already know it won't be our last. No fucking way.

I need more, need to feel her skin under my tongue, need to lap at those perky nipples, need to breathe her in. I need to see her come. I need to smell her release as it drips down my chin.

Reluctantly, I break our kiss so I can fill my lungs with air. She follows me like our lips are connected by magnets. It pleases me to know she's as addicted to me as I already am to her.

I watch as she catches her breath, her eyes closed, lips swollen, cheeks flushed.

"Beautiful," I whisper into the side of her neck before placing a soft kiss there.

Her pulse beats rapidly, which makes me groan and lick the same spot. She bucks her hips, grazing her hot little pussy against me.

"Do you like when I kiss you here, darlin'?" I ask as I continue trailing kisses up and down her slender column.

"Yes," she whimpers, completely lost in sensation.

I growl into her skin, my already hard dick becoming granite at her confession. She tilts her neck, baring the soft flesh to me. I feel like a wolf, needing to sink my teeth into my prey.

Groaning, I nuzzle into her shoulder, taking deep breaths of her now-familiar scent. I know we need to stop, but I can't seem to let her go just yet. Only when Shiloh starts shivering do I finally lean back and untangle myself from her.

"You okay, precious?" I ask, kissing the top of her head.

She gives me a surprisingly shy smile, flushed from head to toe. "There you go again, always asking if I'm okay," she teases. I can sense her nerves, even though she's trying to be playful.

"I can't help it," I admit, pressing a kiss to her forehead. "I always want to know you're safe and happy." Shiloh tilts her head up, searing me with those amber eyes. "And don't ask me why unless you want to tempt me to kiss you again. I don't know if I'd be able to stop this time, though." I had hoped my joke would make her smile, but instead, Shiloh tenses. "What's wrong?"

"Nothing," she lies.

I raise my brow, letting her know I'm not buying it.

"Seriously, nothing is wrong." After a stare-down, she finally rolls her eyes and takes a deep breath. "I just... I've never done... well, much of anything."

I furrow my brow and blink a few times, not sure what she means. But then it dawns on me. "With a man, you mean?" As soon as the words leave my mouth, a jealous inferno blazes right through me. I didn't know I was such a fucking caveman, but the thought of anyone else touching her, kissing her, seeing all of her incredible body on display...

"Yeah, it's whatever though. I don't know why—"

I cut her off with a kiss. This one is gentle, despite the crazy way I'm feeling. I've never been a possessive man, never been known to have a jealous bone in my body. But Shiloh? Fuck no, I'm not sharing her. I'm not letting her get away, either. I'll be the only one to know what she feels like from the inside out. I'll be the one to teach her, to show her how much pleasure she can take.

I sip at her lips, teasing them to part before sliding my tongue inside her wet heat. Stroking the roof of her mouth, I groan when she trembles and gasps. Again and again, I lick into her mouth, exploring her depths and learning what turns her on.

"That's so fucking hot," I breathe out once we break apart. My chest is heaving, trying to suck down more oxygen. Shiloh isn't any better, and it makes me unreasonably happy. "I know it's messed up, but I want to be the only one to touch you like this. I don't like the idea of anyone seeing what's mine."

"Yours?" Her response is barely a whisper, and for a moment, I'm not sure if I said too much too soon. There's no taking it back now, though.

"I'm not gonna hurt you," I promise her. For some reason, I think she needs to be reminded of that, probably a few times. That's okay. I can be patient. "You're safe with me, darlin'."

She doesn't say anything, but she surprises the hell out of me by wrapping her arms around me in a fierce hug. She's still sitting on the table and I'm standing between her legs, as close as I can be. Shiloh buries her face into my chest and I stroke her back, lulling her into a sense of safety.

When she pulls away, I notice a few unshed tears threatening to escape. It guts me to see her like this. I hate seeing her cry, especially not knowing what I did to cause it. "Baby..."

"Before you ask, I'm okay," she says with a little grin and a sniffle. "Just a little overwhelmed I guess." My beautiful girl looks up, those amber eyes fastening onto mine as she studies everything about me. "I don't know what to do with you, Colton."

"Hopefully give me a chance?" I ask, winking at her. She lights up just like I knew she would. So damn adorable. Before she can turn me down, I reach for my phone and hand it to her. "Put your number in." Shiloh scrunches her nose up and I kiss the tip of it, making her giggle. I could listen to that sound every day and never get tired of it.

I watch with a satisfied smile as my girl programs in her number. Her head and her heart are giving her different signals, but at least she's giving me this much. I'll be as patient as she needs, as long as she'll agree to be my wife by the end of the month. That should be enough time for her to come to terms that we're inevitable, right?

As soon as she hands me my phone, I call her so she has my number as well. A deep satisfaction rolls over me and loosens some of the tension in my chest. Now we have a way to contact each other twenty-four-seven. Soon, I hope to be with her night and day, but this will do until then.

"Okay, now git on out of here, cowboy." She hits the *git* just right, sounding like the most adorably grumpy rancher.

"Will you punish me if I stay?" I murmur, leaning in to steal one last kiss.

"No, but I will," a scratchy voice booms over my shoulder. Fucking Joe.

I spin around, glaring at the asshole. I want to say something or possibly knock his teeth out, but I don't think that would go over too well with Shiloh.

"Just helping out with the mess I made," I say casually, giving Shiloh time to gather herself up.

"Yeah, I bet," Joe scoffs. He looks over my shoulder at Shiloh. "That counts for your break today. Now get to wrapping and then come out to the front. We're short-staffed today."

I start to growl at the bastard, but then I feel a warm little hand on my back. Shiloh's soft touch brings me back from the edge. I don't want to make things any harder for her at work. Soon I'll convince her to quit this place. I get the feeling she likes working at the flower shop more, anyway.

Joe stomps out and I turn to face my queen, cupping her cheeks and pulling her in for one last kiss. She fists my shirt, drawing me closer as she melts against me. Fuck, it takes all of my energy to pull myself away, but I need to let her get back to her job. Plus, I have her number now so I can check up on her any time I want.

"I'll call you later, sweetheart," I whisper before kissing her forehead. Shiloh nods and silently watches me walk out of the back room. As soon as I shut the door, I want to rip it off its hinges and scoop my woman up in my arms and carry her away from here.

For now, I'll have to be content with her number and the promise of seeing her soon.

Chapter 5

Shiloh

"You sure you're okay to close up by yourself? Hello? Earth to Shiloh..."

"Huh?" I snap my head in the direction of Cindy, one of the waitresses here at The Shack. Damn, I must have been daydreaming again. It's been a real problem since Colton showed up and gave me my first kiss yesterday.

My lips tingle from the memory and I know I'm blushing. The devastatingly handsome cowboy consumed me, sinking into the kiss and surrounding me with his strength and earthy scent. And when he picked me up and stepped between my parted legs? Good Lord, I thought I was going to come right then and there. All night last night I relived the memory of his hard muscles flexing against my soft curves and the way his hands squeezed my flesh like he couldn't get enough.

"Shiloh!" Cindy says more forcefully, snapping her fingers in front of my face.

"Yeah. Yes. Um...what was the question?"

Cindy rolls her eyes and taps her hot pink nails on the chipped counter. "I asked if you're okay closing by yourself."

I can tell by the way she says it she has no intention of staying to help, but she feels obligated to check in. "I'll be fine. It's been a slow day and I have most of the clean up done anyway."

She hardly waits for me to finish my sentence before dashing to the back room. A few moments later, Cindy walks out with her purse in hand, typing away on her phone. She gives me a wave over her head as she heads out. I don't bother returning it since she's not even looking at me.

I sigh and lean against one of the prep tables, wiping my hands on my apron. I'm kind of thankful to have the place to myself this evening. There are only a few people left in the restaurant, and they'll be on their way soon. Then I just have to sweep, mop, and take out the garbage before balancing the register. It will give me plenty of time to swoon—I mean *think* about Colton.

While my wanton, apparently needy body craves more of his eager kisses and soft touches, my attraction to him is so much more, unfortunately. If he were just a sizzling hot cowboy who made me weak in the knees, I could resist him. Probably. But I'm equally drawn in by his words, the way he holds me, that dang grin that shows off his dimple, and the way his green eyes light up whenever they land on me.

If I were a normal girl, I'd jump in head first and let Colton make good on all of his promises to take care of me. But I'm not. I come with attachment issues and an aunt who likes bleeding me dry of all my cash. What if I gave in to temptation and Colton left? Or what if he took one look at my naked form, curves, rolls, and all, and laughed? It would be devastating. I'm not over one loss, there's no way I could survive another.

So what if his kisses make me light-headed and giddy? And who cares if his touch makes my skin tingle and my bones melt into liquid pleasure? The fact that his deep, rich voice comes to me in my dreams, promising me dangerous things like forever doesn't matter.

None of that changes what I know to be true. My dad couldn't handle me, so he stepped out. My mom was the best person I've ever known, yet she was taken from me cruelly. And my aunt? Well, she's stuck around alright, but only so she can use me.

And yet... a small, quiet voice whispers into my heart, telling me not to judge Colton by the actions of others. That's not fair. But I shut that voice down and focus on work.

I shake my head and finish mopping before turning the open sign off. All that's left is to tackle the garbage and then I can bury myself under my blankets and try to sort out my messy thoughts.

I've already gathered everything up into our two biggest garbage bins. I just have to wheel them out back and pray I can throw them high enough to clear the dumpster in the alley. Usually, I close with either Tim or Chelsea. They're both taller, with Tim being at least six feet. They can reach the top of the dumpster, no problem. Me? At five foot three, it's a bit of a struggle.

Nothing I'm not used to, though. What would life be if not a bunch of obstacles in the way of what we truly want? *Wow*, I need to stop being so melodramatic. I blame Colton. He has my head all over the place.

I shove the back door open with my hip while dragging the first trash bin outside. Thankfully, it has wheels, but it's still a struggle. I wrestle the dang thing out the door, cursing under my breath when one of the wheels gets caught in the doorway.

Finally, I tug the trash can all the way out into the alley, taking a second to breathe after my herculean effort.

Heavy footsteps echo at the other end of the alley. It sounds like two, possibly three people are heading my way. I can't see them from where I'm standing on the other side of the dumpster, but a shiver runs down my spine the closer they get. My stomach turns and all the hairs stand up on my arms and the back of my neck.

I tuck myself behind the dumpster, squeezing my generous frame between it and the brick wall. It's nearly ten at night and I'm alone in an alley with one lousy light that flickers half the time. The other half of the time it doesn't work at all. Of all the nights for a commotion to happen in the alley, why did it have to be the night I'm closing alone?

Straining to hear what's happening between the men, I lean in as close as I dare while still remaining hidden. It sounds like someone stumbles and grunts, and then I hear the sickening thud of a fist landing in someone's face.

Whoever was hit cries out, and I edge even closer, wanting to know what's happening. I'm startled to see a man with black hair face down on the ground, only a few feet from my hiding spot. Then a large hand comes into my frame of view, grabbing the fallen man by the collar and hauling him up.

"Get up, you pussy," one of the men sneers. "If you think that's the worst of what's coming to ya, I've got a surprise."

"Fuck you," the first guy says. He spits out blood and wipes his mouth.

"Ah, no, see, you already fucked us over. Stealing from the boss? What the hell were you thinking?"

"I—"

"No," he cuts the other man off. "What's worse, is I voted for you. I put *my* goddamn reputation on the line. I won't have you ruining my career. I've spent two decades rising through the ranks. You know why that is?" After a moment of silence, I hear a smack, which I assume is another hit to the face. "I asked you a question," he roars. "Do you know how I got to the position I'm in?"

"N-no..."

"By weeding out cheating, lying fucks like you. Now tell me where the money is and I might let you out of this alive."

My jaw drops at the threat, but I manage to cover my mouth before a gasp can escape. Holy crap. The boss? Rising through the ranks? Murder? Who are these people?

"Listen, I'm telling you, it was a misunderstanding," the first man tries to reason.

"Misunderstanding? *Misunderstanding*?" He snorts out a cruel laugh. "Did you hear that, Mic?"

A third man grumbles something. He sounds farther away.

"Yeah, I don't believe it either. I guess I'll have to beat the truth out of him."

I squeeze my eyes shut and cover my ears, blocking out everything about the vicious fight happening just on the other side of my hiding spot. I can still hear cries of pain and the occasional bone snapping. I'm too shocked to cry and too scared to move, so I stay huddled behind the dumpster, waiting for the violence to cease.

"Fine!" someone screams. I assume it's from the man being beaten to a pulp. He rattles off what I think is an account number.

"Did you get that, Mic? Check it out, see if it's there."

"Already there, sir. Looks like he's telling the truth. I'm transferring the funds now."

"Good, good." The apparent ring leader of the group sighs heavily.

"So I can g-go now?"

"Sure, Lorenzo. You did tell us the truth, after all."

"Really?" he squeaks. "Thank you, Trent. Thank you for—"

He's cut off with a click and a bang. Even though I've never heard a gunshot in person, there's no mistaking the deafening sound tearing through the darkness. My ears ring and then pop, my mouth goes dry, and my stomach curdles, but I swallow back the bile and try to remain quiet.

A second later, the body lands on the ground with a sickening thud. I pry one eye open and then slam it shut again. His head is about two feet away from me, the blood from his wounds trickling ever closer.

"Need me to call the cleanup crew?" Mic asks.

"I'm sorry, old friend," Trent says. He truly sounds remorseful, though I can't imagine it's about the life he just took.

"Sorry? What for?"

"I have to cover up my tracks."

"Of course. I'll help. You know I'm loyal."

"I can't have witnesses to this fiasco. Once the money is transferred back, no one will be the wiser."

"Absolutely," Mic says in a shaky voice. "I'll secure the premises."

Silence falls between the two men for long moments. It's only broken when a second shot is fired.

"No witnesses," Trent murmurs before clicking something on his gun. "Shit. Two bodies to clean up," he mutters to himself. "Time to call in a favor."

He whips out his phone and starts rattling off instructions. His voice and footsteps move farther and farther away from me. I know I need to move while he's gone. Who knows how long he'll be away? I definitely need to leave before "the cleaners," whoever they are, come to take care of the mess. They'll for sure discover my hiding spot.

Tears burn my eyes as acid crawls up my throat. I'm trembling and sweating from head to toe. My muscles are so tense, I feel like I can't even move them. I'm afraid I might collapse if I try to stand, and that would draw too much attention.

I take a deep breath, trying not to choke on the rancid garbage smell mixed with tinges of copper from all the bloodshed. Colton's kind green eyes filter into my vision, and I'm surrounded by that feeling of safety from when he held me. As much as I never wanted to depend on anyone, I know I'm in over my head. I just have to get inside to my phone. Then I can call Colton. I have no idea what comes after that, just that my charming cowboy will take care of me.

Summoning all the strength I have, I crawl out from behind the dumpster, carefully avoiding the body sprawled out right next to me. I'm sure I'll be haunted by what I've seen tonight for years to come, but I can't process any of it right now. I'm in survival mode. I don't have the luxury of breaking down, not when adrenaline is pumping through my veins and everything in me is switched to flight or fight mode.

I somehow manage to drag myself to the back door, though I'm still having trouble standing. Using the door handle to pull myself up, I take a quick look over my shoulder to make sure I'm still alone. Well, aside from the slain men who will forever be burned into my brain.

When I'm satisfied that Trent is still preoccupied, I crack the door open and stumble inside. I close the door and lock it, then drag the second overflowing trash can in front of the door to act as a barrier. I know it's not much, but it seems to give me some peace of mind.

My mind is racing, my heart is beating frantically in my chest, and I feel like I'm about to pass out.

Not yet, I remind myself. I need to call Colton. He'll know what to do.

I take a few wobbly steps into the back room and dig in my purse for my phone. My hands are shaking and sweating so badly I drop the dang thing three times before clutching it to my chest. I only have four numbers saved in my phone, so it doesn't take much time to scroll over to Colton's info. Pressing the call button, I hold the phone up to my ear, already feeling better knowing I'll get to hear his voice soon.

"Hey, darlin', are you finished with work yet?"

I open my mouth to respond, but nothing comes out. I try taking a breath and starting over, but all I can manage is a pathetic whimper.

"Shiloh? What's wrong? Are you hurt? Fuck, where are you?"

"Work," I choke out. "I-I-I saw s-s-something—" It's all I can say before my voice is cut off by a broken sob.

"Are you safe where you are?" His tone is different, more severe. This Colton is commanding and in control. He's exactly what I need right now.

"I think so," I murmur.

"What happened? Did you call the police?"

"No!" I say a little too forcefully. "I mean... I don't know what... I..." My breaths become shallow as sweat beads on my forehead and the back of my neck.

"Okay, alright, it's okay, baby," he soothes. "Here's what I need you to do. Take a deep breath and head to the back room, okay?"

I nod my head, but then realize he can't see me. "Yes," I whisper.

"Good girl. Now crawl under the prep table in there. Can you do that for me?"

"Yeah." I drop to my knees, hardly feeling the tile cutting into my skin. Rolling under the table, I manage to curl up in a ball, making myself as small as possible. "Okay, I'm under the table."

"Perfect. You're doing so good, beautiful. Stay on the phone with me. I'm about ten minutes away."

I nod again, but this time I don't have the strength to speak. Colton updates me on where he is while coaching me on breathing deeply and relaxing. Once again, I'm struck by how confident he is in this terrifying situation. I'm beginning to think there's more to my cowboy than just his charm and good looks.

"You hanging in there?"

"Yes," I manage to stutter out.

"I'm so proud of you, Shiloh. Stay right there. I'm pulling up right now. I need to do a sweep of the property, then I'll be right there."

"No!" I nearly shout. "It's not safe. The... the men... the bodies..." I trail off, not sure how to piece it all together.

Colton inhales sharply, then lets out his breath slowly. "Bodies?" His voice is strained, but he's still projecting confidence. "Never mind. I'll be okay, sweetheart. This is what I do for a living. I'm a bodyguard."

For some reason, this makes me laugh. The absurdity of it all. I met this man a week ago, witnessed a horrible crime, and here he is, my own personal bodyguard. Maybe my luck is starting to turn around.

My giggles grow bitter, then uncontrollable. The choppy laughter turns into jagged sobs that scratch my throat on the way out.

"Shh, baby, just a little longer. I'm right here. You feel me, don't you? Feel how safe you are now that I'm here?"

"Yeah," I hiccup. "I feel you."

"Good. You're doing so good, Shiloh. I'll be there soon."

"The door is locked," I suddenly blurt out, remembering the restaurant is closed.

"Don't worry about that. I can pick about any lock there is, darlin.'"

That should worry me a bit, but instead, all I feel is relief. Colton is here. He'll protect me. I needed him, and he dropped whatever he was doing to come to my rescue. I don't have the capacity to process what that means or how it makes me feel.

Chapter 6

Colton

I slip out of my truck, which is parked in the back of the lot, shrouded in darkness. Taking the safety off of my gun, I hold it at my side while moving in the shadows and getting a visual of the situation.

Nothing seems out of place, at first. But I've been in plenty of life-threatening situations that appeared fine to the casual observer. I'm anything but casual, however.

It took every fucking thing in me to be calm for Shiloh during our phone call. The fear in her voice was like a living, breathing thing. Every part of me aches to hold her, but I need to secure the premises first.

I wanted to hound her with questions, especially after she said there were bodies, but I could tell my girl was barely hanging on. Reliving everything so soon after it happened wouldn't have been helpful.

With my back to the front wall of the building, I hold my gun out in front of me and then turn the corner, ready to shoot if there's a threat. I don't see much, so I keep walking. I don't like how dark it is out here. Where are all the fucking lights? I'll need to talk to good ol' Joe and make sure he installs alarms, cameras, and about a dozen more lights.

When I get to the end of the side wall, I see there's an even darker alley sandwiched between two buildings. I don't encounter anyone, nor do I see any bodies. I do, however, see evidence of a shoddy clean-up job. There are splashes of blood on the walls, dumpster, and wooden pallets piled up on one side. None on the ground though, which makes me think they bleached the hell out of it. Sure enough, I take another step closer, and the strong chemical scent hits my nostrils.

Tires spin out, the squealing sound drawing my attention to the end of the alley, where I see a black van pulling away. Sprinting in their direction, I manage to catch a glimpse of the vehicle. All black, dark tinted windows, and most importantly, a pure black license plate. This was a professional job, no doubt about it. But why here? And to what end?

I click the safety on my gun and tuck it into my waistband, covering it with my shirt. The last thing Shiloh needs to see is evidence of more violence. Scrubbing a hand down my face, the wheels in my mind start turning. Who do I know that could give me more information?

I know a few hitmen, but something tells me it wasn't a hired hit. Hitmen are stealthy and calculated, leaving nothing to risk. They certainly don't do a sloppy clean up.

That leaves kidnappers, crazies, or organized crime. My money is on the latter. Good thing I happen to have mob connections as well. Logan always says if he didn't know me better, he'd think I was shady as fuck. It's true, I do have all sorts of questionable connections, but they always come in handy. Half of protecting people is to have all the information necessary to make informed decisions, and hopefully, to prevent anything from happening in the first place.

Right now, my woman needs me. I make a note to reach out to the Moscatellis. This is their territory, and I think Bosco is the capo over this spot. He'll be able to give me some more insight. This doesn't seem like a hit they would carry out, and certainly not so boldly around all these businesses. And if that's true, the Moscatellis need information as much as I do. I might have a thousand connections, but the Mafia has an infinite number of connections and resources.

I complete my walk around the building, just to make sure there isn't still someone hiding on the other side. Once I'm satisfied that I'm alone out here, I head to the front door. The lock is pathetic. Another thing I'll have to talk to Joe about. I'm able to break it with my pocketknife and flick of my wrist. It's a miracle this place hasn't been robbed before.

"Shiloh, sweetheart, it's me," I say as soon as I step inside so as not to scare her.

Taking a quick look around the darkened restaurant, I'm pleased to see it's empty and orderly. Good. No one got in.

I turn around, ready to dash to the back room, when Shiloh flings herself into my arms. I wrap her up in my embrace, lifting her up and crushing her against my chest. My girl is trembling, every muscle wound up tight as adrenaline pumps through her body. She's starting to come down, and soon, she'll crash completely.

"I've got you, darlin'," I murmur, kissing the top of her head. "I'm right here. I won't let anything happen to you."

She nods, tucking her head between my neck and shoulder and wrapping her legs around my hips. I support her weight with a hand under her thighs while my other hand cradles the back of her head.

"I w-was so w-worried ab-bout you," she chokes out.

"Me?" I ask in confusion.

Shiloh nods, squeezing me tighter. "Those men... the blood... what if they hurt you?"

"Shh, sweetheart," I whisper, stunned at her big heart. She was the one who experienced a traumatic event, and here she is, worrying about me. That tells me everything I need to know. She's tried keeping me at arm's length, but deep down she must know we're fated to be. "Let me take you back to my cabin. You'll be safe with me, I promise. We'll figure out the next steps together."

My sweet, brave, scared girl nods again, accepting my help. I know how difficult it is for her to trust, and damn if I don't feel like the king of the fucking world that she's starting to let me in.

"You did the right thing by calling me," I tell her while walking out the front door. "I'm so proud of you, Shiloh," I whisper for the tenth time since she called. I still don't know much about my girl's past, but I get the sense she hasn't had a lot of love and support. That shit stops right now.

Shiloh melts into me, and I can feel the weariness in her aching soul. Loading her up in my truck, I fasten her seat belt and kiss her forehead. Hopping into the driver's seat, I peel out of the parking lot and drive toward my cabin on the edge of town.

With each mile, Shiloh seems to breathe a little easier, though she curls herself up into a ball in the seat, trying to be as small as possible. I place my hand over her knee, rubbing my thumb against her soft skin. She sighs and lets go of some of the tension in her shoulders.

Ten minutes later, I swing into the driveway. My only mission is to get Shiloh inside and make her feel as safe as possible. I don't know what all she experienced, but I'll do everything in my power to protect her and put her at ease.

"I've got you," I say soothingly to Shiloh as I open her door. Scooping her up into my arms, I carry my woman inside, using the thumbprint scanner to unlock the door easily. I promised Shiloh she'd be safe here, and it's not just because I'll be with her. A few months after we started Watchdog, Logan, Slater, and I did some serious upgrading on our building and our homes. Right now, I couldn't be more thankful for the extra security.

I walk straight into the bathroom, knowing more than anything she needs a hot shower. I can already feel her shaking from the adrenaline crash, but first, she needs to clean the day off of her.

Shiloh looks up at me, her eyes rimmed in red as she blinks away tears. The blank look in her golden eyes tells me the reality of her situation hasn't hit her yet. She's still in shock.

"You're going to be okay, darlin'," I whisper, kissing her forehead. I try setting her down on the counter so I can warm up the shower, but Shiloh clings to me, her breathing becoming forced and shallow. It breaks my fucking heart and also ignites a fierce anger deep in my belly. Whoever scared my woman is going to pay. "I'm right here," I reassure her. "Let's get you in the shower, baby. Then I'll get you a clean set of clothes. I promise you'll feel a little more human afterward."

Shiloh looks at me, then looks at the shower, finally nodding her head. Carefully, I set her down on the counter and start the shower. As much as I want to undress her and follow her inside so I can hold her, I don't want to overwhelm her.

Once I make sure she has everything she needs to wash up, I reluctantly close the door, leaning against it. My hands are shaking, every muscle in my body tense with the need to find the threat and eliminate it. That will have to wait until I get in touch with my contacts. I also need to get as much information out of Shiloh as I can. We won't have that conversation until tomorrow, however. It would be too much to bring it all up again right now.

Twenty minutes later, I'm finally starting to relax a tiny bit. I called Logan and Slater to let them know the situation and to tell them I'd be taking a few days off. They both understood. Logan more than Slater, but then again, Slater hardly talks much these days.

Wiping a hand down my face, I take a calming breath, willing the tension to drain from my body. The last thing Shiloh needs is to see me all amped up. I need to be a soothing presence right now. Revenge will come later.

"C-Colton?"

A small, shaky voice draws my eyes toward the hall, where Shiloh is standing in the doorway to the living room. Her face is still a little too pale and her eyes are swollen from all her tears. Even so, she's the most precious, beautiful woman I've ever seen. Especially seeing her in my T-shirt. It hangs down to her mid-thigh, leaving her legs on display for me.

"Come here, darlin'," I say, tearing my eyes away from her bare skin.

Shiloh takes one tentative step forward, and then another. When she's standing right in front of me, she tilts her head down, toying with the hem of the shirt. She tries pulling it farther down her legs, but it's not helping. "The sweatpants were too big," she whispers. Her voice is so damn broken.

"That's alright, sweetheart. Come sit next to me. I'll keep you warm." I try giving her a comforting smile, but I'm not sure I pulled it off.

She nods and takes a seat, her back stiff and rigid. I sling my arm over the back of the couch in an open invitation for her to come closer. I want her to know she has freedom, she has choices, even if she feels trapped in her mind right now.

Thank fucking God Shiloh curls into my side, tucking her knees underneath herself as she leans into me. My girl is trying to be as small as possible while still practically climbing into my lap as if she wants to dissolve into me completely.

I wrap an arm around her, tucking her even closer into my side. She sighs, some of the tension leaving her shoulders as she lays her head against my chest. Combing my fingers through her hair, I tip my head back and close my eyes, breathing in everything about this moment. I think it's the first full breath I've taken since I answered her phone call. Knowing Shiloh is right here in my fortress, right here in my arms, gives me some sweet relief from my panic.

"How are you feeling?" I murmur, kissing the top of her head. She smells like my citrus shampoo, but underneath that is the delicate floral scent I've become addicted to. I like smelling both of us, as weird as that sounds.

"I-I don't know. I'm... I saw... s-so much blood."

"Shh, you don't have to talk about it. Give your brain a break for the night. You've just experienced a traumatic event. Seen things no one should have to see. It's amazing how the brain can heal and make sense of fragmented memories with a good night's sleep. That's the goal for tonight. Nothing else. Just sleep, okay?"

Shiloh nods, snuggling even closer. I can't stand it anymore. I pull her up onto my lap and hold her, rocking my sweet girl back and forth while she clings to me. "How do you know so much about this stuff?" she asks.

I consider lying or coming up with a less depressing reason, but in the end, I know I'll always tell Shiloh the truth. She doesn't trust easily, and right now, I have her trust. I won't go throwing that away for anything.

"I was twenty-one when I was deployed and saw action for the first time," I say softly, running my fingers through her damp hair. It's calming and anchoring in a way I've never felt before.

"Colton," she whispers, turning her head so she can press her lips against my throat. I shudder as unfamiliar emotions roll through me. I've never been in love before, but I sure didn't expect it to feel like this. Raw, vulnerable, exhilarating, and yet safe. "Tell me," Shiloh murmurs.

My woman tilts her head up, those amber eyes glowing with such tenderness it chokes me up. Swallowing the lump in my throat, I continue to bare my soul to the only woman who has ever asked.

"I was in denial at first," I start. "Then the bodies started piling up, one after another, so much so I didn't have time to grieve or be shocked. Numbness was the only way to survive. It felt good, at first. Almost like I was invincible. Nothing could hurt me if I didn't care. But..."

"But that's not who you are," Shiloh finishes for me. I lock eyes with my beautiful girl, feeling seen and understood on a level I never knew was possible. "You've got a big heart. You must have felt each loss so deeply."

I did. Fuck, I still do. I may have a charming smile and the southern drawl down, but I've got baggage just the same as anyone. I thought I was doing a better job of hiding it with a wink and a joke, but this woman sees right through me.

Nodding, I nuzzle into the side of her neck, breathing her in. I know we have so much more to talk about, but not right now.

"Thank you," Shiloh breathes out. "For showing me what's beneath the surface." How does she know me so well already? It's just further proof we're meant to be.

"Anything for you, Shiloh. Absolutely anything."

She turns in my arms, cupping my face in her little hands and resting her forehead on mine. "Anything?" she whispers.

I nod, closing my eyes and letting her scent wash over me.

"Kiss me. Make me forget. Just for now."

I groan and rub my nose against hers, my hand slowly sliding up her inner thighs. "Are you sure? I don't want to take advantage of you, Shiloh." I absolutely want to take everything she's offering, but I would never forgive myself if she woke up tomorrow and regretted anything we did.

"Please? I just want to feel…"

"Feel what?" I murmur, gripping her legs and repositioning her so she's straddling me. I drag my lips up her throat, nipping at her pulse point.

"Just… feel," she breathes out, already lost to my touch.

I slant my mouth over hers, unable to hold back another minute. Shiloh's lips part beneath mine as she slides her tongue into my mouth, immediately taking control of the kiss. She rolls her hips, slowly, so slowly, as she consumes me.

Drinking down everything she's giving me, I slide my hands up and down her thighs, groaning at the softness of her flesh beneath my weathered hands.

"Colton," she whimpers, her breath catching in her throat.

I grip her hips, helping her grind down on me to get the friction she needs. Shiloh moans and arches her back, breaking our kiss.

I kiss down her neck, pulling her sensitive skin between my teeth and then licking the sting away. Shiloh throws her head back, baring even more of her curvy body to me.

Cupping the back of her neck, I draw her back into me for a kiss. Her hands tangle in my hair, pulling at the strands while we taste and explore each other. She's trembling in my arms, but she keeps rocking her hot little pussy against me.

I growl and nip at her bottom lip, pulling it through my teeth before diving back into her sweetness.

"Colton," she pants again, resting her forehead on mine. "I need something... I need something else. I need more."

"I'll give you whatever you want, darlin'," I groan, slipping my hands underneath the hem of the baggy shirt she's wearing. Shiloh sucks in her stomach, which pisses me off. I knead her soft flesh and ample curves, before whispering into her ear, "You're perfect. So fucking beautiful and sexy. Jesus, Shiloh, you have no idea what you do to me. Do you trust me?"

My girl nods eagerly, making me want to beat my chest in pride. I pull her shirt over her head in one swift move, my mouth watering as I take in all of her. She gasps but then moans as my large hands palm her tits.

God, they are exquisite. The dim light coming from the lamp next to us kisses the contours of her breasts, making my dick jerk in my pants. I rub my thumbs over her hard little nipples, and then press her tits together and lick up her cleavage.

"Ohmygod," she whimpers, clutching my hair and holding me to her chest. I grunt as I leave little bites all over the tops of her breasts, kissing and teasing my way down to her pebbled peaks. I suck on her nipples, loving the way Shiloh gasps and writhes in my arms. When I bite down, she squeezes her thighs around me, her entire body locking up.

"You like when I suck your tits, sweetheart?"

"Mmhm... I'm... I'm... I think..."

"Shit, are you going to come for me? Just like this?"

Instead of answering, Shiloh wraps her arms around my head and pulls me further into her, burying my head in between her breasts. I'm suffocating on her and I fucking love it. My hands slide down her back, landing on her thick, juicy ass and squeezing. Hard.

I slide her up and down my lap while meeting her thrust for thrust, dry fucking up into her. Goddamn, I feel her heat through our layers of clothing, feel her need for release, her need for *me* to give her that release.

"I-I-I'm..." Before she can finish her thought, Shiloh cries out, shattering in my arms.

I lift my head up from her chest and swallow down her moans, wanting to taste them while her body pulses with pleasure. My hand slides down her torso, trembling with anticipation. I know she doesn't have any panties on, and the thought is driving me crazy. Shiloh moans and bucks her hips, encouraging me to continue.

I stroke her pussy, barely dipping my fingers inside her slit. Holy fuck, she's drenched for me, and getting wetter by the second. I rub one finger over her entrance and feel her little hole spasm for me. I grunt as precum pours from my angry cock.

I circle my finger over her entrance once more before sliding it up, up, up, and playing with her clit.

"Colton!" she shrieks, digging her nails into my shoulder and burying her face into the side of my neck. "Oh fuck, oh fuck, oh fuck," she chants, her words muffled. Feeling her lips graze against my skin as she circles her hips to the rhythm of my fingers has my balls tightening and drawing up. I know I'm not going to last.

"Let go, Shiloh," I murmur.

"It's too much, too much, I can't..."

"I've got you, sweetheart. Do you trust me?" I ask again.

Shiloh nods and whimpers as I slide one finger into her throbbing channel. Fuck, she's tight. Her walls pulse around me and try to push my digit back out. I press forward, stretching her out as I search for that one spot...

"Oh shit!" she yelps as I rub the rough pad of my finger over her G-spot, again and again. I chuckle darkly at her reaction.

"Love how responsive you are, darlin'. There's so much more where this came from," I growl as I cup her pussy, adding a second finger while my palm grinds into her clit. "Now come for me, baby. Come so damn hard. I've got you."

Shiloh tenses in my arms, her entire body strung so tight as she inhales sharply and holds her breath. I pinch her clit and she snaps, unraveling completely. Shiloh bites down on my neck and I come with her, right in my jeans. Neither one of us can stop grinding into each other as our shared orgasm devastates us both.

Finally, she slumps into my chest, a complete rag doll. I slip my hand out from between us and lick my fingers clean.

"What are you..." Shiloh stares at my tongue while I lap up every last drop from my skin.

"Fucking delicious," I growl, capturing her lips with mine so she can taste herself.

Shiloh moans softly into our kiss and then sighs sweetly when we break apart.

"Holy shit," she murmurs. Then she buries her head into my neck again, as if she's embarrassed.

Yeah, fuck that.

I weave my fingers into her long hair and tug gently, making her lift her head up again. I press my lips to her forehead, her nose, her cheeks, finally giving her a short, sweet kiss on her swollen lips.

"You felt it, too?" I ask, resting my forehead on hers.

She nods and bites her lip before answering. "I felt it. I feel you, Colton."

"Thank fuck." I wrap her up in my arms and hold her close while we soak up the significance of this moment.

Before long, I hear Shiloh's soft little snores. I smile to myself at how adorable she is. I can't wait to wear her out like this time and time again. Hopefully next time it will be with my tongue, followed by my cock.

Chapter 7

Shiloh

I'm surrounded by warmth and a citrusy, leather scent. My brain is foggy and my limbs are so heavy I don't think I can move. Where am I?

Something shuffles behind me and I gasp, suddenly remembering everything. The alley, the gunshots, and Colton coming to save the day. I never wanted to be a damsel in distress, never wanted to rely on anyone for anything. But Colton didn't make me feel weak or foolish.

No, Colton kept telling me that I made the right choice, that he was proud of me, and that I handled everything so well. I didn't know how much I needed his validation. It should scare me, but instead, I feel seen, supported, and maybe even... loved.

As my body wakes up more and more, I'm aware of just how wrapped up I am in Colton. Literally. His leg is thrown over my thighs, his arms are wrapped around me, holding me close to his chest, and his chin is resting on top of my head. It's like he's trying to shield me from every bad thing, and I admit, I kind of love it.

I press a hand to his chest, marveling at the hard muscle underneath his shirt. I don't remember anything after I fell into a coma from my incredible orgasms, but Colton must have carried me in here.

Tracing the defined lines of his arms, pecs, and stomach through the thin material, I feel that aching pressure bloom in my core. The way my cowboy handled me last night, with equal parts roughness and tenderness, makes me crave more. More of his tongue, more of his fingers, more, more, *more.*

I kiss Colton's chest and continue to feel my way down his torso, memorizing every muscle along the way. I trace a path down to the hem of his shirt and slip my hand under, ghosting my fingers over his perfectly sculpted abs.

How can this Greek god of a man possibly find me attractive? The muscles underneath my fingers flex and a low rumbling noise comes out of Colton's mouth.

"Mmm... you feel so good, darlin'. Love waking up to your touch."

I bite my bottom lip as a blush steals over my face. My lust wins out over my shyness, and in a bold move, I run my hand lower, reaching for the growing bulge beneath his shorts. Colton's hand lightly grabs my wrist to stop my motion.

"Don't start something you can't finish, sweetheart." He winks at me, but I can tell he's in just as much pain as I am.

I grin at him, feeling wetness pool between my thighs. "Who says I can't finish?"

He's on me in a flash and before I know what's happening, he has me on my back, straddling me with my wrists held above my head.

"Careful, Shiloh. You're making it hard for me to control myself." He clenches his jaw and shuts his eyes. When he opens his eyes again, there's no denying the way he looks at me. It's a hungry look. "Jesus, seeing you laid out like this gets me so fucking hard. I have to have a taste, baby. You're like every one of my wet dreams come true."

He leans into me, but I stop him.

"Wait!"

Colton freezes immediately and then backs off. "Shit, I'm so sorry. I got carried awa—"

"No, I want to keep going. I promise. I just want to see you first," I tell him with a devious smirk.

The fire returns to his eyes and he grins at me before reaching behind his back and pulling his shirt over his head.

Colton leans down again, this time placing his hands on either side of my head. I reach out and touch his shoulders, slowly dragging my hands down his chest, ribs, abs before reversing my path and pulling him down for a kiss.

My cowboy doesn't miss a beat. He consumes me in a desperate kiss and I get lost in the way his tongue wraps around mine before exploring every inch of my mouth. He swallows my moans before breaking the kiss and trailing his lips down my neck and nibbling on my pulse point.

He leans back and repositions himself between my legs. I instinctively jerk my hips forward, but he puts his hands on my hips to stop the motion.

"Not today, baby. Soon." I pout and he chuckles, leaning forward to bite my bottom lip. "I'll give you what you need, always."

Without another word, he leans back and lifts my shirt over my head. Colton takes my wrists in one hand and guides them over my head again.

"Keep these here for me."

I give him a questioning look. He smiles and leans down, brushing the shell of my ear with his nose and lips.

"Trust me, you'll like it." He nuzzles my neck and kisses a trail over my collarbone and in between my breasts. "Goddamn," he whispers to himself. "I could live right here, buried in your gorgeous tits."

He kisses his way over to my left breast and licks my nipple before sucking. Hard. He groans and releases my breast. Colton continues licking around my nipple and then bites the hard bud.

My back arches off the bed and I let out a sharp cry that turns into a moan.

He looks up at me from between my breasts. "Did you like that, baby?"

I nod, unable to form words.

He growls as he continues sucking and licking. One hand slides up my body, kneading and caressing my sensitive flesh until he palms my other breast. When he bites one nipple and pinches the other, I feel the jolt zip through my body all the way down to my clit. My hips jerk up, rubbing against his hard length.

Colton keeps his mouth on my skin, sucking, nipping, and kissing around my breasts while his right hand trails farther down my body. One finger slips into the folds of my wet pussy tickling me from my wet hole up to my clit. I jerk and moan when his finger circles the sensitive ball of nerves.

"Oh! Colton!"

"I love how responsive you are," he mumbles into my chest.

He kisses his way down my body, pausing to dip his tongue into my belly button. "Are you ready for more?"

I nod my head eagerly, making Colton's eyes blaze.

"Need to hear you say it, beautiful. Do you want me to lick this sweet little pussy until you cream all over my tongue?"

"God, yes," I choke out, fisting the sheets as I wiggle ever closer to him.

"Dammit, woman, you're incredible. I have no control when it comes to you. I'm going to make you feel so good. So fucking good."

A wanton whimper falls from my lips as I spread my legs, showing Colton everything he's asking for. He begins kissing up the inside of my left leg, licking a sensitive spot behind my knee, and placing little love bites on my inner thigh before moving to my right leg and doing the same. He finally gets to my center and I'm shaking with nerves and excitement.

"Relax, baby. This pretty little pussy is soaked for me, isn't it?" He blows over my lips, causing me to jerk my hips. "That's it, beautiful. I want you begging for my tongue."

He spreads my legs farther apart and kisses the soft crease of skin where my legs meet my body. Colton runs his nose up and down both sides of my pussy, driving me crazy. He kisses the soft patch of hair on my mound and breathes in my scent.

"Colton! Please!"

He chuckles and I feel the sound vibrate through every part of me, down to my core. "Please, what, darlin'?"

He uses his thumbs to spread my lips, still not touching me where I need him most.

"Please..."

He blows into my now exposed folds, the sensation overwhelming.

"Please lick me!" I moan, already on edge from his teasing.

He growls. "Gladly."

Colton's tongue dips into my entrance and roams up my slit until he gets to my clit. He sucks the nub into his mouth and I explode.

"Colton, God, Colton..." I moan over and over.

He drinks up my release like he's dying of thirst. He never lets up, bringing his thumb over my clit and massaging the sensitive nerves through my orgasm. He spears his tongue into my hole, in and out, and groans into my pussy, sending vibrations through my core, setting off another orgasm.

"Fuck, Shiloh. You're so responsive, so fucking wet for me. I love tasting you, having your cum on my tongue. Do you like me eating out your greedy pussy?"

"Mmhmm," I stutter out on a shaky breath.

He growls again and doubles his efforts, thrusting two fingers into my pussy while he sucks on my clit. I'm incoherent as I moan and thrash under his skilled fingers and tongue, grabbing his hair and pulling him closer to me, no longer able to keep my arms above my head.

I'm flooded with sensations, every nerve ending on fire. I feel myself gushing all over his hand and I can't bring myself to care. The tension builds in my core. My muscles tighten, preparing for the inevitable release. He bites my clit and I lose it. I scream his name and come. Hard.

Colton licks me again, but I push him away, whimpering, too sensitive. He reluctantly pulls away, breathing heavily.

"Sorry, baby. You taste so good, I can't get enough of you." He crawls back up my shaking body, claiming my mouth in a soul-crushing kiss. I taste myself on him and it turns me on even more. Colton finally pulls away, both of us panting and sweating. He rolls onto his back and takes me with him, draping me over his body.

We both lay there in silence, getting our breathing under control.

"Wow," I sigh, sinking even further into Colton's chest. I'm so utterly blissed out, I'm not embarrassed at all at my little outburst.

Colton chuckles, the sound deep and rich as it rolls over me. "You can say that again, darlin'." I smile at his endearment for me. He makes me feel so precious without even trying. "You okay? I kind of went crazy." A sheepish smile spreads across that handsome face of his, making me feel all warm and fuzzy inside. How is he both adorable and the sexiest man I've ever seen?

"You kinda blew my mind," I whisper back, giving him a grin of my own.

"That's what I like to hear," he rasps before pressing a kiss to my forehead. Colton guides me so I'm lying down on his chest again, my head tucked under his chin as he strokes my back. "Tell me something about you," he says softly.

"Like what?"

"Anything. Everything. I just want to know you."

My cheeks flush at all his attention. It's been a long damn time since anyone cared enough to get to know me. After what we shared last night and this morning though, I know I can trust him. I trusted him to take care of me, not just my safety, but my pleasure. My release. I surrendered more than just my body last night. I'm pretty sure I surrendered my heart. It's his now, which means he's earned the right to my story as well.

"You already know about my mom," I say in a soft voice.

"Yes, I know how much she loved roses and you."

I nod at his words, fighting back tears. Colton kisses the top of my head, silently encouraging me to continue.

"After she... after the funeral, I went to live with my aunt, Margaret. She never seemed to like me all that much, but she gave me a roof over my head and clothes on my back. For a little while, at least. Then she hurt her neck and quit her job. It was one thing after another with her health. First her neck, then her hip, her back, her foot, and basically any and everything that would prevent her from getting another job."

"That must have been a lot of pressure. How old were you?" Colton asks after a few moments of silence.

"Sixteen. I felt bad for her at first, and gladly stepped up and took more hours at Love Blooms. After graduation, the bills just kept piling up and I knew we had no money for me to go to college. Plus, I felt like I owed my aunt or something. But then I found out she only took me in so she could claim my inheritance and drain it all before I got a single penny. I've been trying to dig myself out of the mess she's made ever since. I have dreams, you know?" I didn't realize how defensive I had become until Colton smooths his hands up and down my back, keeping me right here in the moment with him.

"I know, baby. You're so damn resilient and I'm so proud of you," Colton murmurs, nuzzling into the side of my neck.

"Why do you keep saying you're proud of me?" I've wondered that since the first time he said it.

"Because it's true. I see you struggling to keep your head above water, and fuck, baby, I respect you all the more for working your ass off despite the shitty hand you were dealt. That's grit. Determination. Ambition. So few people have that drive, but you've got it in spades, darlin.'"

I look up at him, seeing the truth in his eyes. This man is ruining me. "You really think that?"

"With every damn bone in my body." He leans forward, brushing his lips against my cheek. I'm surprised to find that a few tears escaped, but my gentle giant is kissing them away so sweetly. "Can you tell me what your dreams are? I want to know how I can help."

"Why?" I blurt out. "I mean, why me?"

Colton looks taken aback, and for a second, I think I hurt him. The thought sends a sharp thread of pain through the center of my chest.

"Why... you?" he asks in genuine confusion. "Because I feel you in my soul, Shiloh. I feel you every-fuckin'-where. It's damn cheesy, I know, but one look at those golden eyes and I was hooked."

I giggle, loving the way it makes his green eyes light up. "I'm surprised you were looking at my eyes when I was wearing a freaking hot dog suit," I tease.

"Baby, everything about you draws me in. The hot dog suit just made you easier to find."

I smile at him, soaking up his sweet words. Colton is nothing if not earnest, and I know he means everything he's said.

"In fact, I might need to get you another one," he says darkly, his eyes glinting mischievously.

"I didn't know you were into hot dogs," I say with the straightest face I can manage.

Colton growls playfully and then tickles my sides, making me erupt in a fit of laughter.

"Hey!" I squeal, twisting and turning in the sheets.

Colton finally has mercy on me, settling down behind me and wrapping me up in his arms. "Love hearing you laugh," he whispers, kissing the back of my neck.

"You too," I whisper back, lacing my fingers through his where they are resting on my stomach.

"I laugh all the time," he says with a hint of a smile in his voice.

"Yeah, but today was different. More genuine."

When he doesn't say anything, I worry I offended him. Turning around in his arms, I look up into those forest green eyes. He's staring at me, no, he's staring right down into the depths of my heart, trying to figure something out.

"See? You're perfect for me. You know me better than I know myself already."

"What do you mean?"

"You're right. My default is to be the jokester, the tension relief, the easygoing friend. I didn't realize how exhausting that was until you made me laugh for real. You're amazing without even trying."

He's so sincere, looking at me with something close to awe. It's overwhelming.

Colton must sense things are too intense for me, so he leans forward and kisses the tip of my nose, giving me the biggest smile I've ever seen on him. My big, beautiful, sweet-as-pie cowboy.

"I think it's time I woo you with my cooking skills. French toast sound good?"

"Yes!" I exclaim right as my stomach growls.

Colton laughs, burying his head into the side of my neck and breathing me in. I stroke the back of his head, running my fingers through his hair. Colton sighs and snuggles up closer before pressing a kiss on my throat.

"Okay, if I don't get up now, I won't be able to leave your side all day."

I'm about to tell him I'd be okay with that, but he silences me with a chaste kiss. His gaze turns from playful to somber.

"I need to feed you. We've got a long day ahead of us," he whispers.

I nod my head, knowing he's right. Last night I was terrified, and while I'm still on edge and afraid, the worst of it has subsided just knowing Colton is here with me. He's not letting me go. I don't plan on letting him go, either.

Chapter 8

Colton

"Colton? Haven't heard from you in a while," Bosco says over the phone. He's my contact with the Moscatelli family, arguably the most powerful of the ruling families of Chicago's underworld.

"Ah, but in businesses like ours, no news is good news, eh?"

Bosco grunts, bringing a smirk to my face. I think Bosco could give Slater a run for his money when it comes to monosyllabic, grunted responses. "Does that mean you've got bad news for me?"

"Straight to the point as always." I chuckle.

There's a shuffling on the other end of the line, followed by Bosco's voice, though it sounds like he pulled the phone away from his face. "I'm in here, love."

If I hadn't heard it with my own ears, I wouldn't have believed it. Bosco has a love? I turn the volume up on my phone and strain to hear for more.

"Hi," a softer, feminine voice filters through.

"Come here, little petal," Bosco says. Oh my God. *Little petal*? It's adorable and ridiculous to think about the jacked-up, lumbering captain of the Mafia using pet names on a woman.

The woman giggles and then sighs softly. I shake my head but still smile. It's obvious the two are having a moment. I had heard love struck the Moscatellis hard last year, with the boss, his second in command, and his top enforcer all finding women around the same time. Looks like Bosco did as well.

My mind flashes to waking up next to my precious Shiloh this morning, the sunlight kissing her rosy cheeks and pouty lips. Her little hands slipped under my shirt and she stroked my chest and stomach as if memorizing every dip and curve. Those golden eyes outshined the sun, especially when they landed on mine.

As difficult as it was to tear myself away from her this morning, she needed breakfast, and we needed to talk. I was so proud of her for pushing through her fear and walking me through what she saw. After, I held her for over an hour, simply running my hand up and down her spine while trying to whisper comforting things in her ear.

Shiloh has such a big heart, heavily guarded though it may be. She's strong as hell, and I know she'll get through this, but it hurt so damn much seeing her heart breaking for the violence she witnessed.

I started a bath for her and encouraged my girl to pamper herself while I made some phone calls. Speaking of...

I clear my throat, laughing when Bosco growls and the woman gasps.

"Is there someone on the phone?!" She sounds embarrassed and a little breathless.

"Oh, right," Bosco grunts, clearly not happy to have been interrupted. If I were calling about anything else, I'd just hang up and call back later. As it is, my woman's safety is hanging in the balance and I need him to get started on his investigation. "What do you want?" he growls. The woman says something in the background that sounds a lot like a reprimand. Bosco sighs heavily, making me laugh again.

"Listen, I won't take you away from your lady friend for long."

"She's my wife," he quickly corrects me.

"Congrats, man," I say with all the sincerity in the world. I'm truly happy to see him find love. I know it'll only be a matter of time before I have a wife of my own.

"Thanks. So, what's this about? Anyone in trouble?"

"There was a hit taken out on your territory last night near Wicker Park. You know anything about that?" It's a tenuis line we walk, Bosco and I. He can't answer direct questions about the actions of himself or the family, just like I can't divulge client information. But we know each other well enough at this point to read between the lines.

"Last night? No, that can't be right."

"Trustworthy eyewitness says it is. I scoped the place out as well, just a few moments after it took place. It was a sloppy clean up. More importantly, the van that pulled away was unmarked with a blacked-out license plate."

Bosco hums over the phone, taking it all in. Finally, he takes a heavy breath and lets it all out.

"Well, fuck." He sighs again, and I can picture him running his fingers through his hair.

"Wasn't you then?" I confirm.

He grunts out a no, and I curse under my breath. I didn't think it was, but hearing it has me clenching my free hand into a fist and pounding it down on the desk in my office. I know Matteo, the head of the family, isn't in the business of killing off innocents. If the hit was carried out by one of his men, I know he would promise her protection. Anyone outside of the Moscatelli's won't be as merciful.

"Dammit, no, it wasn't. You think it was another family? Petty criminals? Crime of passion?"

I can tell his mind is racing. The area in question is on his block, and I know he'll be having a conversation with the boss right after we hang up.

"How do you know the eyewitness? Do they have an agenda?"

"The eyewitness..." I debate on whether or not to say anything about Shiloh. Then I remember the goofy-ass way he melted for his woman and decide he'd understand. "Is mine. My woman. She was in the wrong place at the wrong time and saw it all go down."

"She okay?"

I'm relieved that was his first response. "Yeah. She's shaken up. It was the first body she saw, you know?"

"We all remember the first," he says solemnly. This is one of the reasons Bosco and I get along. Despite his profession, he has a heart and feels each loss.

"She's staying with me. We talked about what she saw, and man, I gotta say I think it's a coverup for something."

"Shit," he mutters.

I tell him what Shiloh and I discussed earlier, clenching my fist the whole time. When she told me about the savage beating, the information the man relayed, the initial hit, and then the point-blank murder of the master mind's associate, I could only come to one conclusion.

"A sloppy job by a low-level rival," I finish, giving him my educated opinion. "But I'm still unclear on why or what they were doing on your territory."

"I'll take this to the boss and get back to you," he finally says after a few moments of contemplation.

We say our goodbyes and hang up. I wipe a hand down my face and remind myself Shiloh is safe right here in my cabin. It took some convincing for her to call into her jobs and take some time off. The flower shop owner was very understanding and said to keep her updated on the "family emergency."

No surprise, Joe fired her on the spot. I worried Shiloh would be upset and blame me, but she actually looked relieved. My poor girl has worked herself ragged for years, but that all ends now. No more shitty jobs just to make ends meet.

After regrouping a bit from my conversation with Bosco, I step out of my office to seek out my future wife. I find her curled up on the couch with her nose in a book. I have a feeling I'll be finding her just like this for years to come. The thought calms some of the anxiousness of the phone call.

"Hey, darlin'," I say softly, slipping onto the couch next to her.

Shiloh tips her head up, a sweet little smile curling up the side of her lips. Her amber eyes catch mine, the golden-yellow hues pulling me in deeper and deeper until I'm drowning. "Hi," she whispers, nibbling on her bottom lip.

"How are you feeling?" I ask, wrapping my arm around her and tucking her into my side. Shiloh closes the book and sets it down before snuggling against me. It's the best feeling in the world, having her surrender to my care. Even just this little bit speaks volumes. She trusts me to protect her, enough that my presence makes her relax.

"I'm..." Shiloh takes her time picking out the right words. Another fascinating thing about her. She's thoughtful in everything she does. "Better than I thought I'd be. I'm sure there will be ups and downs when I start processing it all, but right now I'm just... I'm safe." She whispers the last part, but I hear it clear as day.

I dip my head down and capture her lips in a soft, slow kiss. Her words mean everything to me. I always want to make her feel protected and loved. Shiloh opens up for me, stroking her tongue against mine. When the faintest moan falls from her lips, I can't help but deepen our kiss.

Tangling my fingers in her long, dark hair, I angle her head so I can taste more of her. Shiloh responds by gripping my shirt and pulling me closer, throwing her leg in between mine. I choke out a growl and lean forward, pressing her against the seat of the couch.

"Yes," she breathes out in between frantic kisses. I groan when her legs part, allowing me to settle my hips against her core. Shiloh wraps her legs around me, grinding herself against my hardening length.

I bury my face between her neck and shoulder, breathing heavily as I try to keep myself in check. I'm ready to tear her clothes off and sink nine inches deep, but I know my girl doesn't have any experience. I can't let my lust get the better of me and pressure her into anything.

"Why did you stop?" she whines, rocking herself against me.

"Jesus," I groan, pumping my hips against her soaking wet cunt.

She's wearing my big T-shirt again, and nothing else. Her warm juices seep into the fabric of my jeans and I swear to God I almost lose it right then and there.

Shiloh tips her head back, resting it against the couch cushion. She's flushed and breathing heavily, a thin layer of sweat glistening on her throat as she exposes it to me. I lean down and lick the moisture off her skin, growling when she shivers against me.

"Need to... slow... down," I manage to grit out, though that's the last thing I want to do.

"Why?" Shiloh's eyes snap open, her golden gaze doing nothing to hide the fiery need deep in her core.

"I can't take advantage of you."

She looks at me like I'm nuts, and then her swollen lips part into the sexiest goddamn smirk I've ever seen. She's a complete vixen, and she has no idea the power she has over me. "Can I take advantage of you, then?"

"You can do whatever the fuck you want to me, darlin'," I growl. Her eyes flash with a wicked gleam right before she pulls me down for a devastating kiss.

My girl clings to me as she destroys everything I've ever known. Our tongues slide together and then apart, over and over, as our bodies twine around each other tighter and tighter. My entire world shrinks down to just this moment, and I'm completely concentrated on every single place we're fused together.

Finally, Shiloh tears her mouth away from mine. It takes me a second to come back into my body and realign my universe now that she's not kissing me.

When I look down at my girl, she's got the most brilliant smile. I swear she's looking at me with awe. I'm probably looking at her the same way. "I felt it, too," I reassure her. Somehow I just know that's what she needs to hear.

"Show me," she whispers. "Show me what this is between us."

"It's everything, Shiloh. Are you ready for that?"

I rest my forehead on hers, our breaths syncing up. One hand cups her face, my thumb brushing against her delicate cheek, while my other hand slides up her leg and underneath the hem of her shirt.

My girl presses her lips together and peers into my eyes, all while gently rocking her hips against me. I don't think she's even aware she's doing it. "Yes, please," she finally says, giving me the cutest little grin.

I kiss it off her lips and lift her up in my arms, carrying her to my room. I set her down on her feet and slide my hands up her shirt, lifting it off her curvy body. My beautiful girl is standing before me, completely bare. I can't seem to keep my lips off of her for a single second.

Leaning down, I lick a stripe up her neck, then kiss my way back down her slender column, nipping and teasing her sensitive flesh. When I get to her gorgeous breasts, I'm nearly dumbfounded by the perfection I find there. I devour her tits, sucking on her hard little nipples, switching back and forth until she's shaking.

"Oh!" she gasps in surprise, making me growl into her soft flesh and bite down just enough to leave a little mark.

I step back and feast on her incredible body. I can't believe this beautiful creature is offering herself to me, giving me her body, her virginity, and hopefully, her heart.

I gently lay her down on the bed, taking time to admire the soft glow of the late afternoon sun against her pale skin.

"God, you're stunning, Shiloh. So fucking beautiful, darlin.'"

I tuck her hair behind her ear and trail my fingers across her jaw, down her throat, between her breasts, and down her torso, circling them around her belly button. Shiloh giggles, her belly shaking with laughter as she squirms away from me.

"Love that sound, precious," I murmur. Fuck, she's so beautiful. I love seeing her like this, naked, spread out, eyes gleaming with laughter and lust. She's every single one of my dreams come true.

"I want to see you too, ya know. I might not be experienced, but I think both of us have to be naked for this to work."

I growl and tear at my clothes, suddenly needing her skin on my skin, her taste in my mouth, her pussy wrapped around my cock. I take a deep breath, trying to rein it in a bit. This is her first time. I can't fuck her like an animal. Yet.

Crawling over her supple body, I kiss her breasts, the hollow of her throat, her jaw, and finally her lips. She wraps her legs around me and rocks her hips up and down.

"Slow down, baby. I need to make sure you're ready for me," I murmur. My words say one thing, but my body doesn't get the message. I roll my hips in time with her, settling my aching cock along her slit and tapping her clit with each thrust.

"I'm ready," she moans, tipping her head back.

I manage to grip her thighs and pry her legs off of me so I can slide down her body and position myself in front of her dripping pussy.

"Fuck, you are ready. So goddamn wet for me."

Shiloh nods her head frantically, thrusting her hips up involuntarily. I lick her from bottom to top, sucking on her swollen ball of nerves. She's already shaking and panting for me and I can tell she's right on the edge. I reach up with one hand and pinch her nipple while biting down softly on her clit.

She erupts for me, giving me all of her release as I greedily lick up every drop. Shiloh grips my hair and pulls me up, the dark look in her eyes letting me know she needs more. I crawl back up her body, placing sloppy, open-mouthed kisses on her hips, stomach, and breasts. She's writhing underneath me and then moans as I kiss her deeply.

"Gonna pop your cherry with your taste in my mouth. Is that what you want?"

"God yes, stop teasing me, I need you," she whimpers.

I suck on her neck and reach down between us, plunging two fingers into her tight little hole, stretching her out for me. I find her

G-spot easily, groaning when she pulses around me and cries out. I stroke the rough patch of skin over and over until her legs are shaking and she can barely breathe. Right before she comes, I withdraw my fingers and sink inside of her in one long thrust.

"Colton," she yells, coming instantly.

I hold myself still, feeling her orgasm pulse and throb around my cock. She clings to me and whimpers, dragging in shallow breaths until her muscles finally relax.

I look down at her flushed face, a few tears gathering in her eyes and falling. I kiss them away and rest my forehead on hers.

"Are you okay, precious?"

"Yeah... I-I didn't know what to expect but you..." She sighs and opens her eyes, staring straight down into my soul. "You feel good. I'm so full... it's overwhelming but perfect."

"You're perfect, Shiloh. So damn perfect. Can I move?" I grit out, trying like hell to hold on to some semblance of sanity, but she's making it damn near impossible to think about anything else other than pounding her into the mattress and filling her up with my cum.

Instead of answering with words, Shiloh shifts her hips, lodging me deeper inside of her. I growl savagely and bite my lip to keep from fucking her into the mattress.

"Oh God," she breathes out, jerking her hips again to get me deeper.

That's it.

I fucking break.

I pull back and then plunge in deeper. She moans, her eyes fluttering shut as I rock into her, grinding my cock into her sweet pussy and feeling every inch of her ripe, wet heaven. Once I feel her inner walls pulse and beg for more, my control slips completely.

My hips slam against hers and I groan when I see her perfect, round tits bouncing in time with my thrusts. I pick up speed, holding her in place as I take what she saved just for me. The wet slap of our bodies fills the room, along with the beautiful sound of my name on her lips. She rakes her nails down my arms as she drops her head back, completely surrendered to her pleasure.

"So tight and perfect for me. You feel so good, fuck, better than anything I could have ever imagined."

Shiloh moans and crosses her ankles behind my back as she bites my bottom lip and kisses me with ferocious hunger. I grunt and snap my hips against hers, feeling every sweet, sticky inch of her drenched pussy.

"Yes, oh yes, right there," she cries out, arching her back and pressing her tits into my chest.

I dip my head down and rest my cheek against hers as I hammer that spot over and over, loving the sound of her breathy moans in my ear.

"I'm... I'm..."

"I know, love, I feel you. Come for me, Shiloh. Come all over my fucking cock."

Her entire body arches and tenses, expanding before she curls in on herself and screams into my neck, biting down as her orgasm devastates her tiny body. I grit my teeth as cum rises up my shaft, watching as her head tips back and moan after moan pours from her swollen lips. I rut into her, feeling her release another wave of wetness all over my shaft.

I lock my arms and look down at where we are connected. I feel the way we are no longer separate people, but one. That thought tips me over the edge, sending me crashing into an intense orgasm that steals my breath and strength. I shake and pump into her again and again, shooting rope after rope of cum deep inside that convulsing cunt.

My arms give out and I collapse on top of her. I roll over and drag her with me, never breaking our connection as I settle her on my chest with her straddling me. Shiloh whimpers with each exhale, her pussy still quivering around me with little aftershocks.

I tuck her into my chest and stroke her back in a calming gesture, bringing her down gently. We stay like that for long moments, our hearts beating rapidly and then slowing down together. Shiloh is completely limp in my arms, making me smile.

"You okay?" I murmur, not wanting to break this little bubble we're in, but needing to make sure I didn't hurt her.

"So good," she slurs, snuggling deeper into my chest.

I grin and kiss the top of her head, reaching over to grab the blankets and cover us up.

"Me too, darlin'. Me too."

She sighs contentedly and kisses my chest. If I wasn't already a goner for her, that would have sealed the deal. So fucking sweet and sexy.

"I've got you, love. Get some rest now."

Shiloh mumbles something that sounds like I love you, but before I get a chance to ask her about it, I hear her softly snoring.

"I love you too," I whisper.

Chapter 9

Shiloh

My eyes flutter open and a yawn escapes as I stretch lazily. My cheeks flush when I remember where I am, and more importantly, why I woke up in Colton's bed.

I let my eyelids close softly as I picture Colton's muscles flexing above me, his hips pounding against me as he thrust in and out. God, my thighs are slick with desire, which is crazy. I'm still a little sore, but still overwhelmingly turned on. I think I might like the slight sting of having Colton inside me while I'm still fresh and swollen.

What is wrong with me? When did I become this insatiable woman? Then again, if anyone experienced what I experienced with him last night, they'd be obsessed and hot and bothered all the time too.

The comforting smell of strong coffee reaches me, making me sigh and finally get out of bed. I'm still naked from the night before, and can't seem to locate any of my clothes. Reaching for one of Colton's button-ups, I slip it on and do the bare minimum buttons to cover up the essentials.

I've always been more than a little self-conscious about my curves, but Colton made it very clear he loves every inch of me. It makes me want to show off and maybe make him as crazy for me as I already am for him.

Stepping out into the kitchen, I take in the sleek appliances, marble countertop, and hardwood floors. I didn't get much of a chance to check the place out yesterday, but I'm pleasantly surprised to see how open and modern the space is.

I spot Colton leaning against the counter next to the coffee pot, a mug of the freshly brewed liquid in his hand.

"There you are, beautiful," he drawls, showing me that grin I love so much. His dimple pops out, making him impossibly adorable and sexy at the same time.

"Here I am," I repeat, taking a few steps closer.

The man is only wearing loose sweatpants, leaving his sculpted chest on full display. As if in a trance, I close the distance between us, placing my hands on his lower stomach.

Colton groans as I slide them up farther, tracing the contours of his muscles before looping my arms around his neck. Colton groans again, trailing his fingertips up, up, up my thigh and under the hem of the shirt I'm wearing.

I suddenly want more. Need it. Need him inside me, as close as possible. God, my core clenches and throbs as arousal coats my thighs. Biting my lip, I look up into those bright green eyes, my cheeks heating when I get a suddenly dirty thought about my cowboy.

I gasp when Colton spins me around and then dips me low, supporting me with a hand on my back. He ghosts his nose and lips up my neck, pausing to nip the shell of my ear.

"Tell me what you're thinking about that has you blushing all the way down to your toes?" he asks, the deep rumble of his voice vibrating through me.

"You in a cowboy hat," I blurt out, slamming my eyes shut. "And nothing else." *Ohmygod, why did I tell him that?*

Peeking one eye open, I see Colton's darkened gaze, laser-focused on me. He hauls me up into his arms and sets me down on the counter, caging me in with an arm on either side. "You want to ride a cowboy, baby?" he asks with that devilish smirk.

I don't know where this sudden confidence comes from, but I return his wicked smile, loving the way his eyes glint. "Or maybe I want a cowboy to ride me," I whisper.

"Jesus fuck," is all I hear before his lips claim mine.

Colton steps in between my parted legs, deepening our kiss while pressing my body closer, closer, closer. I gasp when he finally pulls away, tilting my head back to get some air. A tortured groan leaves Colton's throat, and he grips the sides of the button-down I'm wearing, ripping it right off of me.

I drop my mouth open in shock and squeal when he picks me up and spins me around, guiding me to rest my hands on the counter. I'm completely naked, bent over, and offering everything to my sweet and sexy cowboy. My inner muscles clench and release, and I rub my thighs together to relieve some of the tension.

"You're killing me, beautiful," Colton grunts, sliding his hands up and down my back. He grips my ass, massaging it and pulling my cheeks apart. A savage sound is torn from somewhere deep in his gut. I feel it vibrating through me, making my heart spike and my knees tremble.

Colton steps into me and places his hands on my hips, covering me with his body. The heated skin of his bare chest presses against my back as his cock brushes against my exposed ass. I grind against him and he sinks his teeth into my shoulder, causing me to throw my head back and moan.

"Goddamnit, Shiloh, is this what you want? Want me to fuck you against the kitchen counter?"

"Yes," I moan.

Colton grunts in approval, and moves his hands from my hips to my breasts, kneading and squeezing them. One hand snakes lower, sliding down my waist and then dipping into my folds.

We both groan as he rubs his fingers over my swollen bundle of nerves. "Colton," I gasp when he plunges two fingers into my entrance, curling them up to hit my most sensitive spot.

Colton continues pumping his fingers in and out while grinding the palm of his hand on my clit. I'm close, so close, so desperately, painfully close.

"Yes, Colton, don't stop, I'm..." Suddenly, he pulls his hand away. "Noooo..." I groan. His absence is painful, my pussy crying out for release. I hear him shuffling behind me, followed by the soft thud of his pants hitting the kitchen floor.

Then, he spanks me. Hard.

"Oh, *shit*!" I moan.

"You like that, Shiloh? Like when I spank you?"

"Apparently," I choke out, making him laugh darkly. He smacks my other cheek and I cry out as the sting travels through my body, setting every part of me on fire.

Colton rubs his cock between my cheeks, then through my soaking folds. He spanks me again and my pussy lips flutter around his dick.

"Fuck, beautiful, you feel so good."

He's working me up again, between the spanking and the head of his cock bumping my clit, I'm about to combust. "Colton, please, *please*, I need to come," I beg.

He glides his shaft along my pussy one more time. I'm almost there. One more touch and I know I'll detonate.

He pulls back and I cry out in frustration until he slams his cock in my entrance in one hard thrust, hitting my G-spot. I come instantly and so damn hard. Colton's arm winds around my waist, holding me steady as I lose myself.

I throw my head back in a silent scream. All the air feels like it's been sucked out of my lungs as my body jerks, my pussy throbbing around Colton's cock, sucking him deeper into me. My muscles tense, squeeze, and release, over and over again. I'm lost, floating in some other world, until Colton's voice brings me back.

"Shiloh, your pussy is eating me up. Fuck, *fuck*, I have to move."

I nod my head, still catching my breath when he pulls out and slams back inside. Again and again, one orgasm rolling into another as he sets a punishing pace.

"Colton... Colton..." is all I can say.

His hands move to my ass, spreading my cheeks apart. "Fucking love watching your pretty pussy swallow my dick, baby. Gets me so hard just thinking about it," he says in a gravelly, breathless voice as he thrusts in and out of me.

Colton drapes his body over mine, his hands finding mine and twining our fingers together. He pistons in and out of me and kisses a trail up my back, over my shoulder, and up my neck to my ear.

"Are you gonna come with me, love? I need you to come with me."

One hand reaches down between my legs and he furiously rubs my clit as he rakes his teeth over my shoulder. My body is completely under his control as he works me over, playing me like an instrument. My muscles grow tight, the pressure in my belly expanding with each thrust, each swipe of his finger on my over-sensitized ball of nerves.

So close, I'm so close, my body vibrating, humming with the need for release, the need for him to break me apart and put me back together.

"Come for me, Shiloh. Come on my big cock. I need to feel you, beautiful."

He pinches my clit and I scream my orgasm, not recognizing my own harsh voice. Colton comes at the same time, his dick pulsing as my dripping wet cunt convulses and swallows every drop of cum he shoots into me.

Colton pulls out and spins me around so my back is resting against the counter. He kneels before me and nudges my legs apart, cleaning me up with his tongue.

My legs are still shaking as he reaches my center. He sticks his tongue in my tight hole, lapping up every drop. He lifts one of my legs over his shoulder as he holds my hips in place. Colton's tongue flattens as he licks up my slit, and I buck my hips when he bumps my clit.

"Colton! I can't, I can't..." I protest. "It's too much..."

He growls, and it echoes through me. There is a feral look in his eye when he lifts his head up, meeting my gaze.

"Not enough, baby. Not nearly enough," is all he says before diving back in.

Colton devours me like I'm his last meal. I didn't think I could come again, but I find myself gripping his hair and shoving him closer, practically suffocating him with my pussy. I don't know where this desperate side of me comes from, but suddenly I need to come again. Need it like my next breath.

"One more, Shiloh, give me one more."

He nips and licks my sensitive nub, batting it around as I squirm in his powerful grasp. Colton sucks me into his mouth and bites my clit.

My back arches as yet another orgasm rockets through my body. I fall forward as my muscles convulse again and again, all of the energy drained from me. If not for Colton holding on to my hips, I'd fall right over.

He swallows down the last of my honey and then looks up at me with a grin, his lips glistening with my release. Standing up, he takes my limp body in his arms and kisses me with such a forceful passion, I have to break away just to catch my breath.

We're both breathing hard, still coming down as Colton wraps me up in his arms, pulling me against his sweaty body. I nuzzle into him, breathing in leather, citrus, and our mixed orgasms. God, it's intoxicating.

"You okay, precious?" Colton asks, leaning back to look me in the eyes.

I blush and nod at him, overwhelmed with how much he cares about my well-being. "More than okay," I whisper, twisting my lips up into a grin. "I think I like it from behind," I confess.

Colton groans and buries his fingers in my hair, tilting my head up to devour my lips. His tongue pushes into my mouth, licking me up in rough strokes. I love it.

"So perfect," he says between ragged breaths. "So goddamn dirty for me, aren't you, precious?"

There he goes again, calling me precious. A girl could get used to this kind of treatment.

"Hmmm," I say with a mischievous smile as I tap my chin. "I don't know. We should probably figure out if I like doing it in the shower too. That way you can clean me up after."

The words are hardly out of my mouth before Colton growls and tosses me over his shoulder. I squeal and giggle, gasping when he smacks my ass.

"You've got me addicted now, Shiloh," he says as he sets me down in front of the shower. "I hope you're ready for what that means."

"I'm ready for everything," I tell him truthfully.

Colton gives me that megawatt smile, the real one I know he only brings out for me. "Good. Now get your ass in the shower, beautiful. Let me see how dirty I can get you."

Chapter 10

Colton

"How's your girl doing?" I ask Logan. He's leaning against the counter in the break room of Watchdog headquarters.

It's the first time I've been back in the office since bringing Shiloh to stay with me. I've checked in over the last two weeks, but I felt like it'd be good to show my face so they don't forget I'm part owner. Plus, I have an update to share with Logan that I'd rather do face to face.

"Spencer is incredible," he replies with a goofy little smile on his face.

I'm genuinely happy for him. He's still a growling, hardass, ex-military man when he needs to be, but Spencer has softened him up a bit. For someone so controlled by routines and details, he picked a woman who is a colorful tornado to be his forever. I think they're perfect for each other and I can't wait for the day Shiloh can meet them. For now, she's holed up at my place until we get an update from Bosco, my contact with the Moscatelli family.

"Good, good," I say with a chuckle, adjusting my old faithful black Stetson.

Logan nods, smiling down at his phone. Oh my God, is he giggling? Spencer is a miracle worker.

He clears his throat and puts his phone away, turning his attention on me. "What about you? Any news about the hit Shiloh witnessed?"

"That's partially why I'm here," I sigh, plopping down in a kitchen chair.

Logan remains standing. Twenty bucks says he'll start pacing any minute now.

"We know for certain it wasn't the Moscatellis, even though it happened on their turf," I start. Logan grunts and starts pacing, right on cue.

"You talked to your contact there? Bobby?"

"Bosco," I correct him, rolling my eyes. Though now I want to call him Bobby and see what the Mafia captain does.

"Right." Logan shakes his head, and I know what he's going to say before he even says it. "You've got a hell of a lot of shady contacts for someone who is on the right side of the law."

"Well, they've come in handy a few times, haven't they?" He grunts, turning on his heel to pace in the other direction. "Anyway. Bosco was looking into it. He called yesterday to say they found the man responsible. Trent. He used to work for the Moscatelli's, but was cast out a few years ago when they were cleaning house. Bosco didn't give me the details, but whatever he did wasn't enough to get him killed, only maimed. The dude has a fake leg and is missing an ear."

Logan pauses to grimace, then motions for me to continue.

"I'll have more information after they interrogate him. I'm guessing he won't be so lucky to get away with a lost limb this time."

I watch Logan process what I've said before he finally sits down across from me. "So your job is done with Shiloh?"

"Never," I reply solemnly. "I'll always protect her."

"Calm down, Colton. I meant, are you available to take on new jobs again? I had to stick Slater on an assignment at a library. I'm sure he's bored out of his mind and would jump for joy at the chance to have you step in."

"Slater jumping for joy? Man, things really have changed around here in my absence."

"Smartass," Logan mutters. "So, what do you say? Will you take on the library gig starting tomorrow?"

"What?" Slater barges into the break room, all seven feet of him taking up half the space. He's breathing heavily and looking back and forth between Logan and me. "The librarian is *mine*." Logan and I stare at him, and I have to make an effort not to let my jaw drop. "I mean the library. The library is mine. My assignment." Slater clears his throat and looks away from us, rubbing the back of his neck.

"Okaaaaay..." I say with a grin. "Well, I very much look forward to having Sunday brunches together in the future with our girls." Logan nods, but Slater just glares at me.

"I don't have a girl," he grunts.

"Soon enough, I'm sure," I respond. No one in the room thinks it was a slip of the tongue that he growled possessively over the librarian.

"Whatever," he sighs, heading out the door. "I don't want to be reassigned. I'm... happy where I am." The broody bastard walks out, leaving Logan and me to gawk at his retreating back.

"Happy?" I mouth to Logan. He looks just as shocked as I am. Slater hasn't been happy in years. I didn't think that word was in his vocabulary. I guess it only took one little librarian to change all that. I can't wait to see how this all unfolds.

"This will be fun," he says, the corner of his lips twitching up into a grin. "So, not the library then. But maybe another client? I don't want to keep using the part-timers and have 'em switch shifts every few hours. Better security if it's longer shifts," he says as if I don't already know.

"As soon as I hear back from—" My phone rings, cutting me off. Sure enough, it's Bosco. "Hey, man, I was just—"

"They got her," he growls. I stand up so abruptly I knock the chair over.

"What do you mean?" I know what he means, but my brain can't seem to accept that anything has happened to my Shiloh.

"The fucker set us up. He had some money scheme going on and wanted to set up a turf war as a distraction. We thought we had him, but it was just one of his lackeys. Even cut off the guy's ear to make him look the part."

"What the fuck?" I roar, taking my hat off and throwing it on the ground. Logan stands up as well, ready to fight the threat with me.

"I know. Listen, we still have bugs at all of their known locations. We picked up some activity in a warehouse down by the docks. At first we thought he was talking to a girlfriend or something when the live feed started playing, but we soon realized it was the witness. Shiloh."

"Jesus... where? What? Goddamnit," I sputter, rubbing my temples. A strong hand grips my shoulder, silently reminding me this is no time to lose my shit. I give Logan a nod, thanking him. Bosco gives me the exact location, letting me know he and his men are five minutes away.

After I hang up, Logan springs into action. "Slater! Get your ass in here," he bellows. Moments later, the big brute appears, looking grumpy as ever. "Colton's girl is in danger. All three of us are going to get her. We'll fill you in on the ride over." Slater looks like he's going to protest, but then his eyes go soft and he nods once. I can't say for sure, but I think he's picturing what he'd feel like if his librarian was in danger.

I don't have my voice yet, so I ball my hands up at my sides and follow Logan out to his truck. I check that I have my gun and knife concealed but within reaching distance on my body. Logan pops open his glove compartment and grabs an extra handgun, tossing it my way. I don't question it, I just take the extra weapon and slip it into my waistband. If shit's going down with a Mafia reject, we'll need all the help we can get.

Slater lumbers out to the vehicle, a slight limp in his right leg. The dude has been through hell and back, but he's just as stubborn and loyal as the rest of us. I know he wouldn't hesitate to risk his life for any one of ours.

I'm bouncing my knee and clenching my fists, the adrenaline pouring over me and gearing me up for a fight.

"Stop fidgeting," Logan grunts. "Your knee is digging in my goddamn back."

But I don't stop. I can't. I'm ready to tear a motherfucker's head off for taking my girl. How the hell did they get into my place? It's a fortress of security. I would have gotten a notification if any of the alarms were triggered. Fuck, I failed Shiloh. I promised I'd keep her safe, and the first time I leave, she fucking gets kidnapped.

"Focus," Slater says, his voice deep and commanding. He doesn't speak much, but when he does, people pay attention. "Channel the fear into determination."

I nod. He's right.

A few minutes later, we glide into the parking lot in neutral, trying not to make a sound. I'm ready to jump out and shoot my way inside, but both Loan and Slater give me a stern look.

Bosco waves us over and introduces us to Rocco, an enforcer, and a few lower-level soldiers. Normally, I'd be memorizing their names and sizing them up to see if they'll be an interesting contact to have in my arsenal. Not today, though.

Focus. Channel the fear into determination.

On Bosco's command, we move forward as a unit, then spread out in pairs. Each pair goes to their assigned entrance, blocking anyone from entering or leaving.

When Slater and I reach the side entrance, I nod for him to open the door and cover me as I head inside. It only takes a few seconds for my eyes to adjust to the darkness, and when they do, my blood boils.

My sweet girl is tied to a chair, tears dripping down her face as some soon-to-be-dead bastard leans over and yells at her. I assume this is the infamous Trent.

"Hot dog girl, I'm talking to you." Shiloh turns her head and he reaches out, gripping her chin and forcefully moving her to look at him. "I know you saw something," he continues, dropping his hand from her chin. His voice is lighter now, like he's having a normal conversation. "I just need you to tell me who else knows. That's all."

Slater wraps his large hand around my forearm, keeping me from lunging at Trent. I know he's right, that I have to play it smart and wait for the right moment to strike, but Jesus, I can't stand to see Shiloh trembling. I especially can't stand some other man's hands all over her.

"Yo, what's over there? Someone here?" one of the suited men shouts, drawing his gun.

"What the fuck are you talking about?" Trent sneers, never taking his eyes off Shiloh. "Gonna need to resort to more forceful methods if you're unwilling to talk, hot dog girl."

"I'm telling you, there's someone here," the man insists.

"Well then go check it out!" Trent yells. "Worthless pieces of shit, all of 'em," he mutters.

I'm not sure who shot first, but it doesn't matter. Bullets fly, the sound cracking and echoing through the warehouse, making my ears ring.

Slater draws his weapon, nicking some guy in the shoulder. He drops to the ground, still alive, but crying like a pussy. I step over him and stride toward Shiloh, my only goal to free her and get her the fuck out of here.

Her wide, terrified eyes meet mine. It rocks me to my core when relief floods her features. Even in the midst of a fucking shoot-out, my woman feels safe because I'm here. I'm humbled and honored that she trusts me like this. Now I need to get her the hell out of here.

I stride toward Shiloh with determined steps. Her eyes flick up, looking over my shoulder. She opens her mouth to say something, her face etched with worry once more, but it's too late for her warning.

Someone grabs my shoulder and spins me around, catching me off guard. It's fucking Trent. The man has a vicious snarl, baring his yellow teeth to me as he reaches for his gun. Others might not notice the slight tremble in his hands, but I've been trained to be aware of every single detail.

He might talk a big game when he knows he has the crushing advantage, but now that he's in a real war against the Mafia, Trent isn't so confident. He looks to his left and to his right, no doubt taking stock of his surroundings. All but one of his men are incapacitated or worse, and the last one is getting the beat down of his life.

Trent snaps his attention back to me. For a moment, I think he might surrender. But then the dumb fuck raises his gun and points it at my chest.

My arm shoots out automatically, knocking the weapon to the floor with a clatter. It spins away as I pounce on the soon-to-be-dead motherfucker, shoving him onto the ground and smirking in satisfaction when his skull bounces off the concrete.

I pause, giving Trent time to see the fury in my eyes. I want him to feel the same helpless fear he instilled in Shiloh. He whines pathetically, pleading for his worthless life, but I'm done waiting.

Blow after blow lands on his jaw, chest, stomach, and anywhere else I can fuck him up. How dare he threaten my woman? How fucking dare he touch her, take her, and make her fear for her life? My rage grows with each passing moment, blood lust and possessiveness taking hold.

"Colton," a soft, sweet voice whispers. I grunt, still lost in my violent vengeance. "Colton, stop. You're going to kill him."

"Good," I snarl, wrapping my hand around his throat and lifting him up slightly, only to slam him back down.

"You can't go to prison. Please, I need you here. I need you."

The voice finally breaks through my haze, and I realize it's Shiloh. She's pleading with me to spare this man's life so I can be a part of hers.

I give Trent one last look, satisfied at the destruction I did. He'll survive, but I know the Moscatellis won't let him live for long. While the alpha caveman in me wants to be the one to eliminate the threat with my bare hands, Shiloh asked me not to. Never mind that there's no way the cops would never get involved in a turf war, thus I'd never end up in prison.

Turning to face Shiloh, I drop to my knees, quickly untying her hands before pulling her down into my lap. The shooting has stopped and the remaining Moscatelli soldiers are in clean-up mode, but Shiloh and I stay locked in each other's arms.

"I've got you, sweetheart," I murmur, kissing the crown of her head. She shivers and sniffles out a whimper that cracks my chest wide open. "Are you hurt, baby?" She shakes her head no, then buries her face between my neck and shoulder. "I'm gonna need your words. Tell me what hurts. What can I do?"

"My wrists are sore, but that's it," she whispers. "I just want to go home."

My heart drops down to my stomach at the mention of her wanting to leave me and go back to her awful aunt's house. Can I really blame her though? I failed to protect her. However, it's still not safe for her to go back, not until I get the all-clear from Bosco that the situation has been completely dealt with.

"I'm sorry, I can't do that," I whisper.

Shiloh pulls back far enough to meet my gaze. Her honey-colored eyes are round and full of tears, hurt painted across her face. "O-okay," she says on a shaky breath. "I understand." Shiloh starts to pull away from me, seemingly caving in on herself. It strikes me then what she actually meant.

"Sweetheart, do you want to come home with me?"

She looks up at me and nods. "Yeah. Home."

"God, I love you, Shiloh," I murmur, kissing away her tears. "I thought you wanted to go back with your aunt. Of course you're coming with me. Your home is with me now." She nods and curls into my embrace.

I stand, carrying her out to the truck. I give Bosco a nod as I load Shiloh into the back seat. He nods back, both of us thanking the other. Like I said, it's good to have all kinds of contacts at your disposal.

"Let's get you home, beautiful," I say, leaning down to press a kiss to her forehead.

"Yes please."

Chapter 11

He's here. Colton came for me, just like I knew he would.

I tilt my head, looking up at my cowboy. He loaded me up in the back of a truck and slid in behind me, pulling me onto his lap. Two other large men get in, making me tense at first.

"That's Logan and Slater," Colton murmurs into the shell of my ear. "They're here to protect you too. We'll all keep you safe. I promise." He looks so broken, and for the millionth time today, I regret leaving the house. I never want to see Colton like this, overwhelmed with worry and completely run ragged.

I don't have the capacity to say anything right now, though. I nod and tuck my head under his chin, melting into his solid chest as he holds me close.

I drift in and out of sleep, not realizing how exhausted I was after everything. I startle awake when Colton lifts me out of the car. "Shh, baby, it's okay. We're home." He kisses my forehead and carries me inside.

When he tries setting me down, my fists automatically curl into his shirt, pulling him closer. I hardly recognize the agonizing sound that falls from my lips. My body seems to be responding on its own, scrambling to be as close as possible.

"I'm right here," he says softly, gliding his thumb over my knuckles and coaxing me to let go of his shirt. "I'm not leaving you, baby. We both need a shower. Then I'll tuck you in bed and hold you until you're not afraid of anything anymore."

Colton's voice trembles on the last word, making me lean back and look into his intense green eyes. He looks ashamed, though I can't figure out why.

"You're here," I repeat to him. "I have nothing to be afraid of."

"Shiloh..." He sets me down on the sink counter, stepping between my legs and wrapping me up in his arms. I can tell he wants to say something else, but he holds it back from me. I think he's more shaken up than I am about the whole thing, which is saying something.

Slowly, silently, he strips both of us of our clothes, leaving them in a pile on the floor before turning on the water. When he's satisfied with the temperature, Colton gathers me up in his arms and carries me into the shower.

"I can walk," I tease, trying to lighten the mood. Colton grunts and sets me down, though he pulls me into his chest, leaving no space between us.

"I know," he whispers. "It wasn't for your benefit. I just need to be near you, touch you, make sure you're here and you're not harmed."

Tears burn the back of my eyes as I curl up into his arms. Colton rocks me back and forth as he strokes my back. We stay like that for long moments, letting the hot water run down our bodies and clean away the dirt and grime from the day.

Colton washes my hair so gently, massaging my scalp with the shampoo and then the conditioner. Once he's satisfied he's washed away all the bad memories, he moves on to the soap. With slow, reverent touches, my cowboy cleans my body, wiping away the fear with each tender stroke of the washcloth.

I kiss the center of his chest, then take the washcloth from him, giving him the same attention. Lifting up one bloodied hand, I carefully wash away the remnants of the attack, then press my lips to his fingers, thanking him for using his strength to defend me.

Colton reaches out with his other hand, cupping my cheek and guiding me to look at him. "Sweetheart..." he whispers, his voice clogged with emotion.

"I know," I tell him softly, placing my hand over his heart. "But we made it. We're okay." We're so connected in this moment I can practically hear what he's thinking. Our little paradise of the last few weeks was infiltrated, and he's scared we won't get back to that same place.

Colton scoops me up, toweling us both off hastily before laying me down in bed. He crawls in next to me, turning on his side so we're face to face. "Talk to me, beautiful. What are you thinking? What are you feeling? How can I help? God, what can I do?"

Each word is more panicked and rushed than the last, and I reach out, covering his mouth with my hand to stop him from spiraling completely. The shocked look on Colton's face is enough to draw out a little laugh. His eyes soften, making me absolutely melt for him.

"I'm thinking it's a good thing I fell for a protective cowboy bodyguard," I answer with a little grin as I drop my hand from his face.

Colton's face drops. "It didn't do you any good when you needed it," he mutters. "How did they get you?"

I sigh and curl up on his chest, embarrassed by how stupid I was. "No one broke in, if that's what you're thinking. None of this is your fault," I reassure him.

"It's not yours either, baby. What happened?" Colton combs his fingers through my hair, letting the wet strands fall lightly onto my exposed back and shoulders.

"You're always cooking these amazing meals, and I wanted to surprise you with dinner for once. Obviously, I didn't think it all the way through. I just wanted to show you..." I trail off, feeling stupid and torn open for Colton to see. I remember the way he held me the first time we met, how he didn't shame me or make fun of my costume. Colton's only goal was to take care of me, just like it is now.

"Show me what?" he whispers, brushing his lips against my temple.

"How much I... well, how much I love you." I hold my breath and squeeze my eyes shut. Colton tenses, making my stomach drop. Shit, I shouldn't have led with that.

"You love me?"

"Yes," I respond right away. "It scares me how much sometimes. You barged into my life and refused to walk away, and now..."

"Now?" Colton breathes out, hanging on my every word.

"Now I wouldn't let you walk away if you tried," I say with a smile. His green eyes flicker with playfulness, a look I'll always cherish. It was a traumatic day for both of us, but I knew my cowboy would come for me. Seeing the flash of light in those endless eyes lets me know we're going to be just fine. We both still have some things to work through, but for now, having each other is enough.

Colton nuzzles into the side of my neck, inhaling deeply as he presses my body closer to his. "I love you so damn much, Shiloh. I've loved you forever. I don't know how that's possible, but the second I saw you, I knew. You were always a part of me, and fuck if I'm ever letting you go now."

We lay like that for a long time, tangled up and naked, soothing each other and healing together. The sunlight filtering in through the window turns from bright yellow to burning orange, then fades into purple as night falls.

Colton gently rolls me to the other side so he can spoon around me. His hand traces over my hip and lifts my top leg over his. I feel his rock-hard cock slide into my entrance. Everything is so much more intense in the dark, my other senses heightened. Colton hisses as he pushes himself further into me, so slowly.

I moan when I feel him hit my womb, and then he starts pulling out slowly. He keeps up the excruciatingly slow pace, building us up one stroke at a time. I press back against him when he pushes in, and I squeeze around him when he pulls out, creating the most exquisite friction.

His hand spreads out over my lower belly, keeping me pressed close against him and tightening that pressure already gathering at my core.

Colton rests his head on my shoulder. His muscles tense as he controls his movements, commanding both of our bodies with his steady rhythm. It's a slow burn, but I feel the fire catching, licking at my nerves, sending a rush of heat between my legs.

"That's it, fuck, baby, love being inside of you, love how wet you get for me." He picks up his pace slightly and my muscles spasm with each thrust. "So goddamn tight. You feel incredible, love. Are you there, baby? I need you to come for me."

He thrusts once, twice, three times and I convulse in his arms, squirting all over him and trembling from my orgasm.

"Jesus, you made a mess, baby girl. I fucking love it." He pounds into me, rubbing my clit with his fingers, one orgasm tumbling into another as he fucks into me, pushing me higher and higher.

"Shiloh, fuck, Shiloh..." he chants over and over, his cock swelling and exploding inside of me. The force of his release triggers a final, deep orgasm to break out over my body.

I curl in on myself, so sensitive from all of my orgasms. Colton just holds me in his arms, thrusting lazily as we both come down.

"I've got you, beautiful, I've got you," he whispers as he nuzzles his head into my hair. "Thank you, love."

We fall asleep like that, with Colton still inside of me.

Chapter 12

Colton

"How's the flower shop?" Spencer asks Shiloh. "I bet it's magical to work with all the beautiful flowers. So many colors!" Her eyes go wide as she smiles brightly. Logan throws his arm over the back of her chair, tucking his woman into his side.

"It really is," Shiloh agrees, before launching into the newest shipments and her favorite arrangements she's worked on during the week.

I watch my beautiful girl laugh and swap stories with Spencer, and a feeling of complete joy and peace fills me up. This is exactly what I pictured the moment I saw her in that damn hot dog suit. Okay, I'll admit I also thought about ripping the costume off her body and bending her over the nearest surface, but giving her an adoptive family of sorts is good too.

It's been two weeks since Shiloh officially moved into my place. Our place. Her aunt was none too happy, but I wrote her a check for five thousand dollars and said that's the last handout she'll be getting. There was no love lost between Shiloh and her aunt, and I only wish I would have taken her away from that hell hole sooner.

I lean back in my seat, surveying the messy remnants of a delicious meal. Spencer invited everyone over for dinner, including Slater. I was surprised when he showed up but in a good way. He's not one for social events, and I thought he might be even more skittish with new people around. I wonder if his librarian has anything to do with him coming out of his shell a little bit.

My eyes fall on Logan, who is giving Spencer the happiest, goofiest grin. The man is wrapped around her little finger, and he doesn't look one bit upset about it. I get it. I treasure every word out of Shiloh's lips and am grateful for every moment we're together.

We both had nightmares for the first week after the kidnapping, but we've talked through a lot of the lingering fears and insecurities. I know there will be more challenges ahead, but we're solid and I've made sure my girl knows I'll always be here for her.

A gruff sound at the other end of the table pulls me from my sappy thoughts. I look over at Slater, who appears to be typing out a text. It only takes me one guess to figure who he's talking to. Oh shit, was that his laugh? Is the big growly brute flirting?

Logan notices too, catching my eye and grinning. I shake my head, returning his smile.

"Ready to go, sweetheart?" I ask Shiloh. Her cheeks flush and she nods her head, biting her bottom lip. I have to concentrate far too hard on not groaning or laying her out on this table so I can eat her up.

She's been so turned on lately. Like all the time. Not that I'm complaining, but it's a lot of responsibility to pleasure your woman exactly when and how she needs it.

We say our goodbyes, and as soon as Logan closes the front door, I toss Shiloh over my shoulder and run to my truck.

"Hey!" she says with a giggle.

"Sorry, not sorry," I grunt, giving her ass a little smack. She gasps and squeezes her thighs together. Jesus, this woman is going to kill me.

I speed home, not fast enough to put us in danger, but certainly faster than the signs posted on the side of the road. I have Shiloh inside and pressed against the wall as fast as humanly possible, her body rolling against mine in search of release.

"Fuck," I growl into the side of her neck, nipping her skin and licking her there. "Never get enough of you."

Shiloh nods her head and I lift her up into my arms, pinning her against the wall. I grind my obscene erection into her center, loving the way it makes her squirm. I'm about to lose my damn mind with the need to be inside her, but Shiloh presses against my chest.

As much as it kills me, I set her down and take a step back. I never want her to feel pressured or uncomfortable around me. "Everything okay?" I ask after a moment of collecting myself. Shiloh nibbles on the corner of her mouth, not quite meeting my gaze. "Sweetheart?"

"I... yes. I think. I have something to tell you," she blurts out. My girl looks flustered and a little anxious.

"Whatever it is, we'll face it together," I say soothingly, trying to take away the worry in her eyes. Shiloh nods and then takes my hand, leading me over to the couch. Is she going to tell me we're moving too fast? Fuck, is she going to leave me?

"So..." Shiloh starts, plopping down on the couch and twisting her hands in her lap. I reach out, covering her hands with one of my own. She gives me a little smile and takes a deep breath. I'm on the edge of my seat, literally, waiting for this woman to crush me. I've never felt so vulnerable. I know without a doubt I'd never recover if she decided to walk away from me. From us.

"You're killing me here, darlin'," I drawl, trying to ease some of her tension.

Shiloh looks up at me with those magical eyes. Doubt and hope swim around inside her endless golden gaze, and I wait until she lets hope win out.

"I'm pregnant," she whispers.

It doesn't hit me at first. It's too perfect. Surely I can't get everything I've ever wanted in such a short amount of time, right? The woman of my dreams, pregnant with my kid, living with me, and soon to be wearing my ring.

"I-I know we never talked about it, and, well, I-I mean, I know we never used protection, but I just... I just..."

I realize I've just been sitting here, staring at her, slack-jawed. My brain finally kicks in and I smile so wide my cheeks hurt.

"We're having a kid," I whisper, cupping her beautiful face in my hands and kissing her forehead. "God, you're perfect."

"You're okay with it? I didn't know if—"

"If I was in this forever? If I'd want the love of my life to grow big and beautiful with my child? Darlin', you've just made all my dreams come true."

"Really?" she murmurs, looking up at me with glassy eyes.

"Well, almost," I say with a wink. Her brow furrows in confusion, her bottom lip sticking out in the slightest hint of a pout. Fucking adorable. "There's just one last thing I need you to do for me."

"Okaaay..."

I kiss the tip of her nose and dig into my pocket for the little box I've been carrying around for weeks now. Pulling it out, I open the black velvet box and present what I hope is an acceptable wedding ring. "Wear my ring. Be my wife. Have all of my children."

"All of them? How many are we talking here?" Shiloh whispers through tears. Her smile is brilliant as her eyes sparkle brighter than the diamond ring. I slip the ring on her finger before she can protest. Good thing she doesn't.

"Maybe a baker's dozen?" I tease, leaning in for a kiss. Shiloh is still looking at the ring. Thank God with awe and not disappointment. She's distracted momentarily as she studies the setting and rose gold band. "I'll take that as a yes?" I whisper before kissing her cheeks, nose, and finally, her lips.

"A baker's dozen, huh?" she pants once we break apart.

"We can start with just the one though, don't worry." Shiloh laughs and I capture the sound with a long, passionate kiss. "But first, say yes." I whisper the words onto her lips, gently biting down on the bottom one.

"You didn't give me much of a choice, cowboy," she says, rolling her eyes playfully. "But yes, I suppose I can marry you and give you between one and thirteen kids."

"Good girl," I growl, taking her lips for my own.

She moans into my mouth and I trail my lips down her jaw, her neck, her collarbone. I gently push her back so she's lying down on the couch and continue my trail of kisses down between her perfect tits. I can't wait to see them swell up. Fuck, now that I'm thinking about it, I can't wait to see her pregnant.

My lips slide down her ribcage and then I lift up her shirt and kiss her belly. Resting my forehead there, it finally clicks into place. This is everything. We're starting a family together. She's fucking mine, all mine, and now she's tied to me in every way.

I close my eyes when I feel Shiloh's fingers weave into my hair and massage my scalp. "You're growing my baby in there," I whisper against the soft skin of her belly before kissing it again.

"Yeah." She giggles.

"That's so fucking sexy," I growl. And it is. Jesus, I want nothing more than to be inside of her right this fucking second.

"It is?"

Instead of answering her, I hook my thumbs into the waistband of her leggings and panties, peeling both of them down her legs to reveal her perfect, pink little pussy. Without any warning, I dive into her sweet perfection, licking up her slit and circling her clit.

Shiloh cries out in surprise at the unexpected invasion, but soon I taste her arousal. I suck and lick and nip at her folds, her thighs, her hard little clit. She's soaking me, my face sloppy with her juices. I fucking love it. She comes hard and fast, her pussy pulsing around my tongue as I lap up her release.

"Again," I growl into her tight, hot cunt.

Shiloh moans as her hips buck, grinding herself against my mouth. I grab her hips and pull her even closer until I'm suffocating inside her sweet heat. I lick her clit again and again until my tongue is numb. She sucks in a huge breath and then cries out her climax. I crawl up her body and kiss her, hard and deep. She takes everything I give her, moaning at her taste in my mouth.

Not wasting any more time, I rip her shirt down the middle and unhook the front clasp of her bra, removing both items of clothing in under a minute. Shiloh giggles at first, but then moans as I suck one breast into my mouth. She bows her back off the couch, thrusting her chest further into me. I kiss and lick my way to her other breast and give it the same attention.

I leave her briefly, only to unbuckle my belt and pull off my jeans and underwear. I grab one of her ankles and place it over the back of the couch while the other one rests on my shoulder, spreading her wide open for me. Looking down at this stunning woman, chest heaving, pussy dripping, eyes fogged over with lust, I can't help but groan.

"So fucking beautiful. God, you're perfect, Shiloh."

I line myself up and enter her tight little channel in one long thrust. I growl, just feeling her come again, needing to show her how much I love her, how I'm never leaving her.

"Mine," I grunt as I piston in and out of her.

"Y-yours, oh, fuck, fuck, Colton, I can't hold on…"

"Let go, Shiloh. I love watching you come. I love hearing you come. I love feeling you come all around me. So come for me, darlin'." Her orgasm slams into her, causing her body to shake and convulse beneath me. "Goddamn, Shiloh, Jesus Christ, that's it."

I fuck her through her orgasm as she whimpers and writhes. I can't hold off much longer, but I don't want this to end. I want to be inside of her forever.

I pull out of her as she moans, snapping her eyes open and searing me with her lustful gaze. Standing up, I pull her into me and spin her around, guiding her to lean over the arm of the couch. I grab her hair and push her forward onto her elbows. I press my cock against her soaking wet pussy, her previous releases dripping down her thighs. I tease her as I wait for the exact right moment.

My cock spurts cum at the sight of Shiloh bent over the couch for me. I grit my teeth and take a calming breath, trying to keep my shit together. I need her to come one more time. Ten more times. A thousand more times. But for now, I'll settle for her fourth orgasm of the day.

"Colton, please, please get inside of me."

"Fuck, baby, you know I'll always give you what you need."

I tease her a little longer, rubbing my cock up and down her slit. When she starts shaking and whimpering, I slam my thick dick deep inside of her, triggering another orgasm. I roar with pride over how much pleasure I can give my woman, and how well she takes all of my many inches.

My hips snap as I buck and thrust, my heavy balls slapping her pussy. Every time we join together, we make the most obscene and glorious wet smacking sounds. It makes me impossibly harder.

I can't tell if she's having one long orgasm or if she's had five more, but her pussy has been squeezing and snapping around me the entire time. I loop my arm around her waist, holding her up just as she starts to collapse. I give one more hard thrust before fucking exploding inside of her.

It's so intense, so fucking everything. I keep emptying into her, coming harder than I ever have. Each rope of cum feels like it's taking a part of my very soul, draining me and pouring more of me into her. I'll give her everything. There is no me without her.

Finally, fucking *finally*, I'm completely spent. I curl my body over hers, covering her back with my front as I kiss the back of her neck, loving the salty taste of her sweat.

Shiloh is shaking in my arms, panting and sweating and well-fucked.

"You okay, sweetheart?" I whisper into her ear.

"I... fuck," she breathes out. "S-so good. Can't feel my legs."

I chuckle and then stand up, pulling out of her swollen, soaked pussy. Spinning her around again, I scoop Shiloh up into my arms. She's a rag doll, and I chuckle again, kissing her forehead before collapsing on the couch with her in my lap.

She curls up into my chest and rests her head in the crook of my neck.

"I love you, baby girl. Nothing will ever change that. You are my family, my home, my whole damn world. I'll do whatever I can to prove that to you."

She nods and kisses my neck. "I know," she whispers into my skin. "I know that. I was just scared it was all too good to be true, you know? But I want this more than anything. And I want it with you."

We sit like that for God knows how long, the air thick with sex and promises of forever. It's the most perfect moment I've ever experienced, and I know it's just the beginning of our story.

Epilogue

Shiloh

I wake up surrounded by soft blankets and Colton's leather, citrus scent. I roll over to see if I can wake him up the way I did yesterday morning—with my lips wrapped around his morning wood—but he's not here.

I stretch and take my time getting out of bed before throwing a robe on and wandering out to the kitchen. I pause at the coffee maker, wanting my morning cup, but then smile, remembering why I'll be skipping it for a while. I opt for a glass of orange juice instead, taking it with me as I head to the living room, where I hear Colton talking on the phone to someone.

"Yeah, Amy was a colicky baby too. I used to hold her on my forearm with her belly facing down until she finally fell asleep," he says.

I assume he's talking to Logan, who just got home from the hospital with Spencer and their second child. Hearing the two ex-Marine bodyguards swap parenting tips warms me up body and soul, causing me to smile.

Colton looks up and sees me leaning against the entrance to the living room. He smiles brightly, a genuine smile, and motions for me to come closer.

"I'll talk to you later, Logan. Congrats again and try to get some rest," Logan grunts, making Colton roll his eyes.

I skip over to him, feeling light and fuzzy all over. I can't believe this is my life. Three years ago, Colton swept me off my feet, hot dog suit and all, and he hasn't let me go since.

"How are you feeling today, darlin'?" he asks, nuzzling the back of my neck and kissing my there. I sigh and melt into his embrace.

"So good," I answer honestly.

His lips pull into a smile against my skin while his hand finds its way to my belly. He can't seem to stop touching me there ever since I told him I was pregnant with our second child two days ago. He also hasn't stopped doting on me, carrying me around, massaging my feet, feeding me, and otherwise spoiling me. I never thought I'd want a man to take care of me, but Colton doesn't make me feel weak or taken advantage of. In fact, he lets me take advantage of him all the time.

"That's what I like to hear." Colton sits up a little, adjusting me so I'm sitting sideways on his lap with my legs stretched out to one side. "How did that big order of flowers go at the shop?"

I smile and launch into a story about a client with an over-the-top fairy tale wedding. The bride was stubborn and a little entitled, but I took the challenge head-on and delivered exactly what she wanted.

Colton's bright green eyes glint with pride as he listens to me finish up my story. He's been nothing but supportive of me taking over more responsibilities at Love Blooms. Right now, I'm in a trial period as part owner, soon to be full owner if all goes well.

"As long as you're not working too hard," he says, kissing my temple. "I need all my girls to be happy and healthy." Colton rubs my belly and kisses the tip of my nose.

"You're so sure it's a girl, huh?" I ask with a smirk on my face.

"Mmhm," he murmurs, brushing his lips against mine. "I'm hoping for twins," he whispers.

My jaw drops and I'm about to tell him that's easy to wish for when he's not the one giving birth, but he cuts me off with a kiss. I can't think when his tongue slides against mine or his hand slips underneath my robe, stroking my bare thigh.

We break apart when Amy's little cries float through the baby monitor. She just turned two and we've been having a fun time figuring out a new sleep schedule.

"Let me get her," Colton says, helping me off his lap. "You stretch out and I'll be back with coffee."

"I can get her, you got up with her during the night."

"I'm not keeping score, darlin'. We're a team and you deserve to relax this morning. Let me take care of my girls."

His sweetness causes me to tear up, though I try to blink them away. Colton hates seeing me cry. He's kneeling by my side in a second, looking stricken. God, this man.

"You can't just say romantic things like that and expect me not to bawl!" I scold him while wiping my tears. "You know I'm a mess of hormones right now."

Colton cups my face and kisses my forehead. "And you know I won't ever stop telling you how much I love you."

"I guess we're at an impasse here," I sniffle, giving him a little smile.

My big, sexy cowboy swoops in for a kiss, lifting me up in his arms. I squeal as he carries me down the hall and into Amy's room, setting me down in front of her bed.

Our little girl stops crying and lifts her chubby little arms up. Colton scoops her up and then turns to me, wrapping an arm around my shoulders and holding both of us against his chest.

He lets out a contented sigh before kissing Amy's head and then mine. "Love my girls," he whispers.

"Love you, Daddy!" Amy shouts enthusiastically. She bursts into giggles when Colton tickles her with his beard.

"Love you," I say, looking up at him with such awe. This man has given me a home, a family, and a happily ever after fit for a storybook. In this case, the reality is far better than fiction, and we have forever to write the rest of the story.

THE END

Also by Cameron Hart

Check out my other popular series and books!
Mafia, MC, & Bodyguard Romance:
<u>Moscatelli Crime Family Series</u>[1]
<u>Di Salvo Crime Family Series</u>[2]
<u>Chaos MC series</u>[3]
<u>Savage Ride</u>[4]
Mountain Man Romance:
<u>Men of Blackthorne Mountain Series</u>[5]
<u>Bear's Tooth Mountain Men Series</u>[6]
Cowboy & Small Town Romance:
<u>Roped in by Love Series</u>[7]

---

1. https://books2read.com/u/mqBaze

2. https://books2read.com/u/m0odzW

3. https://books2read.com/u/bMVAOk

4. https://books2read.com/u/bMVlG7

5. https://books2read.com/u/3RYDvB

6. https://books2read.com/u/mVel7A

7. https://books2read.com/u/3RYlBY